Christmas Carol

& THE SHIMMERING ELF

Also Available

Christmas Carol & the Defenders of Claus

Christmas Carol

& THE SHIMMERING ELF

By the author of Christmas Carol & the Defenders of Claus

ROBERT L. FOUCH

Sky Pony Press
New York

First Edition

This is a work of fiction. Names, characters, places, and incidents are from the author's imagination and used fictitiously.

Sky Pony Press books may be purchased in bulk at special discounts for sales promotion, corporate gifts, fund-raising, or educational purposes. Special editions can also be created to specifications. For details, contact the Special Sales Department, Sky Pony Press, 307 West 36th Street, 11th Floor, New York, NY 10018 or info@skyhorsepublishing.com.

Sky Pony® is a registered trademark of Skyhorse Publishing, Inc.®, a Delaware corporation.

Visit our website at www.skyponypress.com.

10 9 8 7 6 5 4 3 2 1

Library of Congress Cataloging-in-Publication Data is available on file.

Cover design by Kate Gartner

Cover illustration copyright © David Miles

Print ISBN: 978-1-5107-5099-9

Ebook ISBN: 978-1-5107-5101-9

Printed in the United States of America

For Mom and Dad

CHAPTER 1

All Alone, Nobody Home.

If the elf known as the Ancient One hadn't yanked me into a portal, I would be gone.

Not dead.

Gone.

As if Carol Glover had never existed.

I never would have lost my mom or dad, or lived with my cold-hearted uncle, or become best friends with a girl named Amelia, or helped rescue Dad, or become a Defender of Claus and saved Santa from the uncle who betrayed me. None of it would have happened. But the Ancient One, also known as my grandmother, saved me.

And I am thankful she did, even though the world we reemerged into was a terrifying place.

The two of us were visiting in her cozy cabin at the edge of the elf kingdom. Actually, we were doing homework. Or I was. Now that I lived in the North Pole, Grandmother had taken it upon herself to be in charge of my "schooling." Which meant math problems and geography lessons and quizzes on government and history and science. It also meant reading, lots and lots of reading.

It's not that I don't like to read—I love to!—but I prefer exciting stories with adventure and magic and danger, or stories that make me laugh. Grandmother certainly lets me read books like that (Santa has a huge library of classics), but she also insists I tackle stuff like William Shakespeare (soooooo boring), and Charles Dickens (not just *A Christmas Carol*, unfortunately) and Mark Twain (not *too* bad), and Harper Lee (OK, I have to admit, Scout and Atticus are awesome!).

And now I was reading *A Wrinkle in Time*, a super intense book about a girl named Meg who travels across the universe with her genius baby brother and a friend named Calvin to save her father and defeat a dark force trying to take over everything. I was really getting into it, with the magical Mrs. Whatsit, Mrs. Who, and Mrs. Which, and the creepy pulsating brain of IT. But that day in the cabin, I didn't feel like "schooling." Only four days remained until Christmas. I should have been on vacation already! And I also knew that when I finished, I would have to write a report (ugh) and then pick another book out of the stack Grandmother keeps on her living room table.

We sat next to a crackling fire and sipped hot cocoa, a drink I had turned down but Grandmother brought me anyway because elves *really* love their sweets! I couldn't concentrate on *A Wrinkle in Time*, distracted, as I often was, by thoughts of the Masked Man, the bad guy who turned out to be my Uncle Christopher. Nearly a year had passed since I'd defeated him, and I still couldn't get over what he had done. He betrayed his own brother, the niece he was supposed to take care of, *and* Santa! I could never understand it, and I obsessed over it, which drove Grandmother batty.

"Where do you think he is?" I asked.

Grandmother sighed and spoke to me telepathically. *I have no idea, dear. Read your book, please.* Elves, in case you don't know, communicate without speaking. And though I was only part elf, I had the telepathic ability, along with other powers that came from my potent mix of elf and Defender blood.

"Or he's plotting his revenge," I responded aloud, pretending not to notice what she said about the book. I set it on the table to see if she would let me get away with it. I picked up my cocoa, pushing aside my wooden Santa figurine, the one my parents had given me and one of the fifty-nine Santas in my collection. I'd brought it from my room at Santa's house to help decorate Grandmother's cabin. Even with Christmas so near, she wasn't overly excited about decorating—"It's always Christmas in the North Pole!"—but I insisted on making her home appropriately festive. (My nickname *is* Christmas Carol, after all.)

Three stockings had been hung by the chimney (with care, naturally): one for me, one for Grandmother, and the other for Dad. A small tree in the corner was weighed down with so many ornaments that Grandmother feared it would collapse. The tinsel I'd strung around the room made the cabin sparkle. Mrs. Claus had found a miniature ceramic Santa village, and it sat on a table surrounded by

4

cotton snow. I was definitely in all-out Christmas mode, but that had the unfortunate effect of making me obsess about my uncle even more. I sipped my cocoa, trying to wash away the bitterness of his betrayal.

"You can't worry about your uncle, dearest," Grandmother said, speaking aloud for the first time that day. She knew how, having spent years in the human world, which of course is how I came to be. "No one's reported any unusual use of Defender power."

I eased back in my seat. She said nothing about the discarded book. Maybe I was done with homework for the day. Mission accomplished! "Dad says he vanished from his job at International Toy." Both he and my uncle have Defender powers like me, able to freeze time (helpful for Santa to deliver all his toys in one night) or make powerful blasts we call North Pulses. But my uncle chose to use his powers for evil, building a toy empire with the goal of eliminating Santa.

"He's probably afraid you'll find him and kick his butt," Grandmother said, winking as she blew the steam off her cocoa. I picked up my cane, which Grandmother had given to me and was carved from the wood of an ancient elven forest she once explored. The magical cane was a weapon I used to focus my powers, but it was painted with red and white stripes, disguised as an oversized Christmas ornament to hide its true nature.

Suddenly, Grandmother bolted upright in her chair. The drink flew from her hands. The cup shattered. Scalding drops splashed my ankles, making me leap off the couch and spill my own drink, which soaked *A Wrinkle in Time*. My cane clattered to the floor.

"What's wrong?" I picked up the cane and held it close, sensing its pulsing power. I always felt safer with it in my possession.

Grandmother held up a gnarled finger to shush me. The cocoa dripped from the table. She closed her eyes and placed her other hand to her head to concentrate. Without saying a word, her eyes popped open. She made a circle with her hands to create a portal, an opening through time and space that elves use to travel from one place to another in an instant. Moving faster than I'd ever seen her move, she threw her arms around me and pulled me toward the portal. "Jump, Carol!" We leaped in. The crackling fire and Christmas decorations, the spilled cocoa and the pile of books, they were all a blurry vision when I turned to look. In an instant, the living room vanished. I rubbed my eyes, wondering if the portal was playing tricks on my vision. What you saw from inside a portal was distorted, but it was real. And the living room was no longer there; only blackness.

What's happening? I shouted in my mind.

The fear I sensed in Grandmother terrified me.

Something terrible, she answered. *A huge disturbance.*

We floated for the longest time, just waiting. Portals are hot, humid places. Everything moves as if in slow motion, everything's a struggle, like being underwater. I had never been in a portal for so long. *I need to get out! I can't breathe!*

Hold on, dear. You have to hold on.

I couldn't understand why she was doing this. Where were we going? Who were we running from? How was drifting in a portal, feeling like I was about to die, helping anything? I thrashed around, desperate for air. I kicked my feet as if swimming, moving toward the portal opening.

Not yet! Grandmother screamed, and she locked her arms around me, trapping me with her elven strength. I struggled against her. If I didn't escape at that very moment, I would pass out and I feared I'd never wake up.

When I didn't think I could take it any longer, dizziness overcoming me, Grandmother screamed, *Now, Carol!* and we kicked toward the portal opening. I still could see no living room, no light from the crackling fire, no books or wooden Santa. Where had it all gone? With a final kick, we plunged through the portal. Cold air washed over us. I hungrily sucked in oxygen as we collapsed into knee-deep snow. I leaped to my feet. The cabin was gone. It was dark, but the clouds covering the full moon were drifting away, the snow glowing in the moonlight.

"Carol," Grandmother said quietly. "Look." I turned and nearly fainted. The elf kingdom, that intricate city of beautiful blue ice, full of sliding, telepathically chattering, Santa-helping elves was gone! All that remained was a ruin—toppled houses, crumbling slides, smashed ice statues, everything covered with snow. And the massive tree around which the kingdom had been built was splintered down the middle, half of the tree on the ground, the other half hanging limp.

"Nooooo!" I screamed, my voice echoing in the emptiness. "What happened?"

Grandmother's ancient body sagged, as if the weight

of the centuries she had lived suddenly fell upon her. "Someone went back," she said softly.

"I don't understand."

"Someone traveled through time and changed the past, which changed the future."

"Who?" But I had already guessed who; I had no doubt about who. "I mean, how?"

Before Grandmother could answer, something horrible occurred to me, a thought so awful that, once again, my head swam. I turned and ran, leaving the Ancient One standing alone in the snow. "Carol!" she called. *Carol! Come back!* But I kept running, so panicked that I forgot I could have made a portal to where I wanted to go. The snow was deep, and my legs burned. I stumbled into the dark woods between the elves' kingdom and Santa's house, falling twice over branches and stones under the snow. I emerged into the clearing where I had once practiced with my magic cane and accidentally destroyed the lone tree that grew in the middle of the field. I was stunned to see the tree standing tall and proud, as if what I remembered had never happened. I gripped my cane to reassure myself that it existed, that I wasn't hallucinating.

I breathed a sigh of relief when I spotted the giant reindeer barn, its peak silhouetted against the moon-lit sky. At least *something* hadn't changed. But there were no lights. There was no movement. I sprinted past the barn and toward Santa's front gate. The house looked the same until the moon emerged from another passing cloud. The picket fence had collapsed. The mailbox that received every child's letter to Santa leaned sideways. The front porch roof had caved in on one side. The swing from which I'd watched Santa and the Defenders leave on Christmas Eve a year ago lay broken on the porch. Boards had fallen from the side of the house. Windows were shattered. There was a large hole in the roof.

Then I spotted it, a wisp of smoke from the chimney. My heart soared. I ran to the front porch and saw a glimmer of light inside. "Dad!" I yelled. "Santa!" I ran up the stairs, nearly falling when my foot crashed through the broken first step. I burst through the front door and stopped short at the sight. The room was lit with only a barely smoldering fire. Shadows danced like wicked creatures on the walls. To my left were the shelves of toys, a sort of museum display of Santa's long history of bringing joy to children around the world. But only the top shelf was full, showing the earliest toys like straw dolls and wooden wagons. The other shelves held no G.I. Joes or talking dolls or video games or any other modern toys. Dust covered everything. White sheets draped the furniture. If not for the fire, the house would have appeared abandoned.

A soft clearing of the throat broke the silence. "Who's there?" The feeble voice came from an ancient wooden chair I recognized as Santa's "throne," as Mrs. Claus called it, teasing the old guy as only she could. The chair was turned away from me, toward the warmth of the fire.

"It's me," I said, inching closer. "It's Carol."

After a long pause, the man in the chair said, "Carol? I don't know any Carol."

I stopped at that. What was happening? Nothing made sense. "But I live here," I said. "With my dad. With Santa."

"Impossible," came the voice. "Santa's gone. He's been gone for a long, long time."

I screwed up my courage and took the last few steps to see the man in that chair. His face was buried in his hands. But he had a long white beard. His hair was wild and unwashed. He wore red pajamas. A blanket lay on his lap. A half-eaten piece of bread sat on a plate on the table next to the chair. "What do you mean he's gone?" I asked. The man said nothing. He didn't look up. He didn't take his hands from his face. All he did was let out a long, soft groan. "Are you OK?" I asked.

The man yanked his hands from his face and jerked his head toward me. His eyes were crazed. His face was gaunt and skinnier than I'd ever seen. Though he looked like a different person, I had no doubt this was the man I'd dedicated my life to protecting as a Defender of Claus. "Santa?"

The man launched himself from the chair and I jumped back. "I told you!" he screamed. "Santa's gone. All that's left is me. Just me. Poor old Nicholas. All by his lonesome." Then he laughed a terrible laugh that scared me more than anything else I'd encountered on that dreadful day. Santa wasn't right. Nothing was right.

"Stop it!" I yelled.

And Santa laughed again, his eyes dancing crazily in the firelight. "All alone. Nobody home. All alone. Nobody home."

"I said stop it!" I shouted and slammed my cane on the floor. A North Pulse blasted Santa back into his chair. Sparks flew from the fire, lighting up the room. Furniture toppled. A cloud of dust exploded, making me choke and cough. Santa buried his face in his hands and cried softly. I rushed over and threw my arms around him. "I'm sorry. I'm sorry. I didn't mean to."

In the glow from the firelight, the air shimmered. A portal appeared with Grandmother on the other side. She dove through and landed with a thud in front of me. "Too old to be jumping through portals," she grumbled, wiping dust from her robe. "Goodness, I'm a wreck." Then she noticed her surroundings. "Oh my."

Santa looked up at the Ancient One, his eyes wide. "You're an elf."

"I most certainly am," Grandmother said.

"Why did you all abandon me?" Santa asked.

"I did nothing of the sort," Grandmother snapped. "Where are the elves? Where is Mrs. Claus?"

"Gone," Santa said. "For ages."

"And what about the Defenders?" I asked, desperate to know where Dad was. And for that matter, Mr.

Winters, the man who had recruited me to become a Defender.

Santa looked at me as if I were speaking an alien language. "What are Defenders?"

"What do you mean?" I asked. What was wrong with him? "The ones who protect you!"

Santa laughed again, this time with bitterness. "No one *protected* me. Why do you think I'm alone up here?"

"Carol," Grandmother said, nodding toward the door. "Let's talk outside. Excuse us, Santa."

"It's Nicholas," he said and sank back into his chair. "All alone. Nobody home," he muttered. "All alone. Nobody home."

We walked out to the front porch, and Grandmother gazed at the empty reindeer barn. The doors stood open, one hanging crooked from broken hinges. "What's happening?" I asked, my voice crackling in the silence.

The old elf looked at me with fear in her eyes. A chill tickled my spine and worked its way into my heart. "I think your uncle went back in time and stopped the Defenders from ever being formed. He changed history."

"Then where's Dad?"

"I have no idea, Carol. There's no way of knowing. All of our memories, everything we think of as reality, none of it may have happened. Maybe he was never even born."

I felt dizzy and leaned on my cane. "Then how am I still here if everything's changed?"

"I sensed it," Grandmother said. "There was a massive shift in the time-space continuum, like being in a plane as it hits turbulence. That's why I pulled us into the portal. I kept us outside the continuum while he traveled back. So we weren't affected by whatever changes he made."

I tried to wrap my mind around what she was saying, but it made my head hurt. "So what do we do?"

"I don't know, Carol." Grandmother sighed, glancing at the house in which poor Santa sat staring at his lonely fire.

"We go back and fix it!" I said, filled with rage. I used to feel sorry for my uncle; he always seemed lonely and sad. But no more! He was an awful man who had escaped my grasp once. I would not let that happen again. "How do we travel back?"

The Ancient One pondered this, and I thought I might explode with impatience. I had to act! We were wasting time. But I breathed deeply. I needed to let Grandmother think. She was the wisest being I knew, and I trusted her with my life. After all, she had just saved it. "Your uncle couldn't have managed this alone. I know of only one elf who has mastered time travel."

"Who? Where is he?"

"He was kicked out of the kingdom because he became obsessed with time, with going back to the moment something terrible happened in his life."

"He tried to change it?" I could sympathize with that. My own mother died when I was six. What I wouldn't give to go back and hug her one last time, or to try and save her.

"Yes. But I don't have time to tell you that story now. We must find him." Finally, I thought, we were taking action. "Let me concentrate," she said, and she put her hand to her head and closed her eyes, searching for the long-lost elf. Less than a minute later, her eyes popped open. "Let's go."

"You found him already?"

"It wasn't hard. I traced the source of the time disturbance. If it's his doing, that's where we'll find him." She made a circle with her hands, creating a portal.

"What about Santa?" I asked, looking back at the light flickering in the window.

"That's not Santa," Grandmother responded, shaking her head. "Not the Santa we know." I took her outstretched hand. I closed my eyes. Together we dove through the portal, off to rewrite history.

CHAPTER 2

Back to New York

The Ancient One and I emerged into the darkness of Central Park, the most secluded place we could think of in which to make a portal and not be seen. Grandmother said New York was the site of the time disturbance, and she was certain that's where we would find the guilty elf.

I was back in Manhattan! The place I'd met Santa, where I had agreed to become a Defender and my life changed forever. Only this time everything was all wrong. And it might never get fixed. Was I really the only Defender left?

Grandmother and I fell into a snowdrift in the park. The cold and ice doesn't bother me much since, as a Defender, I was built for the cold and even feed off it. But

I still don't like getting my clothes all wet. Grandmother landed upside down, her tiny feet sticking out of the snowbank, her cries for help muffled as I pulled her out. "I'm too old for this nonsense," she said, brushing herself off. She was quite the sight, with her long silver hair and a blue robe that made her look like a fashionable monk. I wondered how we'd get around the city without drawing attention to ourselves.

"Where do we go now?" I asked, shaking snow from my hair.

"Downtown," she said.

"How do we get there?"

"The subway of course."

"But I don't have any money."

"Carol, dear, sometimes I wonder if the battle with your uncle knocked a few screws loose. Just follow me."

We wandered through Central Park, keeping to the shadows. The park was surprisingly empty, aside from a late-night jogger, a patrolling officer, and a scruffy-looking fellow who I guessed was homeless. I felt sorry for him and wished I actually did have money to give him. I checked my watch (Santa-themed, naturally), which Dad had given to me the previous Christmas. *9 p.m.* Thinking of my father, I tried not to cry. Did he exist in this world or had my uncle snuffed out his own brother? I shuddered at the thought.

I first noticed the stares in the subway station. At Grandmother, yes. But mostly at me! I assumed it had to do with the white stripe in my red hair, the mark that indicated I possessed Defender powers. But most of the world doesn't know what that means, so maybe the people staring just thought the stripe was odd. Was I really that strange, especially in New York City, where you could see all kinds of bizarre-looking people? Passersby would glance at Grandmother, then look at me with wide eyes, hurrying away as if I were a rabid dog.

What's going on? I said telepathically. Grandmother had pulled her hood over her silver hair. We approached the turnstile for the Downtown train.

I don't know, she answered. *Something's definitely off.*

I know I'm weird-looking but come on, I said, smiling. But Grandmother just glanced worriedly at the panicky people.

Freeze time, the elf commanded. A subway officer inside a glass booth watched us.

Why?

Grandmother sighed. *Just do as I ask, please.* I might be a powerful Defender who had saved Santa Claus, but Grandmother possessed her own special power: the ability to make me feel like a dope with a single sigh. I waved my hand through the air to manipulate the strands of time we Defenders can control. I'd gotten good at it, particularly with the help of my cane, which focused my powers. Everyone in the station froze. The subway officer stared, unmoving. A train pulling out of the station stopped. Exiting passengers were locked in mid-stride. That's when I noticed something strange about them. They all wore the exact same clothes, a plain gray full-body jumpsuit, like a factory worker might wear. Women, men, children, it didn't matter. They all had on the same bland, ugly uniform.

Grandmother climbed over the turnstile and I steadied her as she landed stiffly on the other side.

"Look how everyone's dressed," I said as I hopped over. The ordinary sameness of everyone gave me goose bumps. Not the good kind.

"Very strange indeed," Grandmother said.

As we approached the open train door, I caught a glimpse of something at the end of the platform. "What is it, dear?" Grandmother asked.

"Someone moved."

She looked alarmed and hurried onto the train. "Start time!"

I moved my hand. The world sprang to life. The subway doors closed and the train pulled out of the station. At the end of the platform where I'd seen the movement stood a young boy, maybe a year or two older than me, wearing the same gray uniform as everyone else. He stared into the train. Our eyes locked. He took off his winter cap and I gasped. The boy had blazing red hair and running down the middle was a long stripe of white. The train plunged into the darkness of the tunnel and the boy was gone.

On the train, more stares—at my hair, at my cane, at our clothes, at the ancient lady no one could possibly know was an elf. I avoided eye contact with everyone, but a nervous-looking man dialed a cell phone, glancing repeatedly at us and whispering into the phone.

We need to get off this train, I said.

Grandmother stood and we waited at the door, holding on to the pole as the train bumped into the station. When the door opened, the man rose to follow. I stopped. He hesitated, and now I knew for sure he was following us. I listened for the *ding* indicating the door was about to close. I waved my hand near my waist, making a small circle, gathering up the strings of time and space. When the bell dinged, I stepped onto the platform. The man followed. I aimed a North Pulse at his chest. It was a little one but enough to knock him backward. The door closed, the train took off, and I hurried after Grandmother up the stairs and onto the streets of Manhattan.

I immediately realized where we were: 49th Street! As we hurried through the crowd in Times Square—even tourists wore the same dull uniforms!—Grandmother produced a winter cap. "Hide that hair."

"Where did you get this?"

"Never mind that."

I put on the cap and stuffed my long hair underneath, wondering if Grandmother had just shoplifted a hat. We waded through the teeming crowd, many of them gawking up at the Times Square lights. At least that hadn't changed. The tourists made me think of New York's biggest attraction during the holidays. "I want to see the tree."

Grandmother sighed again. "You really do have a screw loose, dear. We don't have time."

"Please. I need to see it. I need to make sure that hasn't changed."

The Ancient One started to argue, but she saw the look in my eyes. Her shoulders slumped. "Lead the way."

We pushed through Times Square, but as we neared Radio City Music Hall, things changed. There should have been a mass of humanity heading toward the tree and the skaters and all the Christmas decorations. But the crowd had thinned to just us and a few others. And I gasped when I saw Radio City. The building was dark. In fact, it looked abandoned, and the marquee read: "Closed until further notice." No Radio City Holiday Spectacular, no Rockettes, nothing.

I stopped a passerby. "What happened to the Christmas show?"

The man stared at me blankly. "I don't know what you're talking about," he said and hurried away.

"We have to get to the tree." My best friend Amelia and I had walked these streets a year ago, exhilarated by the prospect of seeing that beautiful tree. Now I took the same steps filled with dread. The streets were nearly deserted as we approached the square that held the tree and the skating rink. When we rounded the corner, I thought I might be sick. I couldn't breathe. My eyes welled with tears.

"Where is it?" I asked. Before us was emptiness, a giant gray slab of concrete with a couple of benches and a lamppost in the middle. No towering spruce twinkling with lights, no ice-skating rink, no happy tourists oohing and ahhing at the winter wonderland.

"You know what happened, dear," Grandmother said softly. "He changed it."

"But how? How can everything be so different?"

"That's what we need to find out. Come, we must go."

We retreated into the shadows, the streetlights dull and murky away from the Times Square bustle. I heard the scrape of feet and froze. Shadows darted this way and that. The strangest feeling came over me. I tried to turn to the danger that was closing in. But I couldn't move. I saw them coming, two scraggly boys, aiming something at me. Grandmother said in my mind, *I'll come for you, dear.* She slipped into the shadows, made a portal, and vanished. After that, I saw no more.

When I awoke, I thought for sure I was in a cave. In New York City? But then I saw the platform, the graffiti, the tracks, and realized I was in a sort of manmade cave, a subway station, long abandoned by the looks of it. Candles burned everywhere, shabby furniture was strewn around the platform, and a lone lamp with a bare, burning bulb cast huge shadows. I was handcuffed by my left wrist to an old turnstile, my cane was gone, and I still didn't feel quite right. I tried waving my right hand to make a North Pulse, but I felt nothing.

"That won't be working," came a voice from behind me. I turned to see a boy with brown hair that had been dyed poorly, traces of red showing through, and I wondered if he possessed the power. He had dark eyes and dressed like the rest of the people in this world. But his uniform was dirty and ragged. He was tiny, probably a foot shorter than I was, and so skinny I imagined he might disappear if he turned sideways. His accent was thick, not Spanish like Amelia's. Maybe something European or Russian.

"Who are you?" I asked.

He leaned over me. "Your worst night dream," he growled. I didn't mean to, but I laughed. The boy looked shocked, then annoyed. "What is your problem?"

"I think you mean *worst nightmare.*"

"This is what I stated."

I laughed again. "OK."

He flinched as if I'd insulted him. "I'm on charge now. Remember that."

"What?"

The boy muttered to himself in a language I didn't recognize. "I'm on charge!" he yelled.

"Oh, you mean *in charge.*"

"Yes, in charge."

"Of me?"

"Yes, of you."

"That's good to know."

"We will not bring you harm."

"Who's we?"

"He will explain."

"Who's he?"

"Never mind that."

"Where are you from?"

"America, of course," the boy said, crossing his arms on his chest.

"Um, OK." I didn't really care. I just wanted to know who he was, who he worked for, and why I suddenly couldn't use my Defender powers. "What is this place?"

A soft voice came from the shadows. "Home. Who are you?"

I tried to find the source of the voice, but the subway station was too dark. "I should ask you that question," I responded, trying to sound tough.

"I don't think you're in a position to be asking questions." He waited for a response, and when I hesitated, he said, "We don't want to hurt you."

"But you've done something to me. I don't feel right."

"So it's true. You didn't dye your hair that way and dress funny just to get attention." At last the voice emerged from the shadows. The boy with the white stripe in his hair! He'd been on the platform when we pulled out of the station. "You have the power, right?" he asked. His red hair was trimmed tight against his scalp, and he reminded me a bit of Amelia, his skin the same beautiful brown. He was handsome, even in plain gray. I felt myself blush and hoped the murkiness of the station hid my glowing cheeks. I nodded. If he was going to hurt me or turn me in to my uncle, he already would have.

"All with power have been found by them," the other boy said.

The boy with the white stripe sighed. "Let me do the talking, Ivan."

"Do not reveal names!" he hissed. He turned to me. "Ivan I am not."

"It'll be fine," the other boy said. "My name's Ray. You're not going to tell anyone about us, right?" He looked at me with the slightest of smiles. I had no idea what his intentions were, but I liked him. I couldn't help it. I even liked Ivan-I-Am-Not, goofy as he might be.

"I don't even know who I'd tell. I'm not from here."

"From the United States?"

"It's hard to explain." That's when I noticed, in the far corner, a drawing on the wall. A man with a white beard and an odd red hat. Underneath, on a small stack of crates, was a crude doll that looked a lot like the drawing. Next to that stood a drooping tree, covered with makeshift ornaments made from scraps of metal, shards of colored broken glass, and other pieces of garbage you'd pick up off the street. Surrounding the display were flickering candles, along with flowers left in front like offerings at a shrine. My heart swelled. There was no mistaking who that was supposed to be. "Santa," I said, a tear darting down my cheek.

Ray stepped forward excitedly. "You know who that is?"

"Of course," I said. "Santa Claus."

Both boys gasped. "How do you know that name?" Ray asked.

"I'll tell you if you let me go and tell me who you are."

The boys huddled together, whispering feverishly, until at last Ray turned to me and nodded. He pulled a key from his pocket and unlocked the cuffs. He pointed to a weird-looking contraption behind me that resembled a laser gun from a cheesy old sci-fi movie, only bigger, and with a boxy metal base. "I'm leaving that on."

"What is it?"

"It messes with our power. It's how he stops the ones who don't join him."

"Who?"

"What do you mean who? Do you live in a cave or something?"

I laughed, looking around at the gloomy station. "Actually, I think you do."

Ivan-I-Am-Not laughed, too, until Ray shot him a dirty look. "Tell me how you know about Santa," Ray said.

I hesitated. Could I really trust these boys? They had, after all, just tracked me down with some kind of Defender-nullifying machine and kidnapped me right off the street. And if I told them what had happened to me and how history itself had been altered, would they even believe me? I looked into their dirty, skinny faces, and you know what I saw? In the world where Santa was no longer Santa, where Christmas wasn't Christmas and everything

I knew had changed, I saw belief. I saw hope. I took a deep breath and told them my story.

When I finished, the two boys stared at me for the longest time, saying nothing. Then they laughed, wild crazy laughter, the kind that makes your sides hurt. My cheeks burned and I imagined they were as red as the stripes in my missing cane. "What's so funny?!"

Ray wiped his eyes. "Elves? Defenders? Presents from Santa every Christmas? Hahahaha!"

"I'm telling the truth!"

"Right," Ray said and got up as if to leave. "I have things to do."

"I can prove it."

"Mm-hmm." He kept walking.

I concentrated on making a portal, hoping that the contraption blocking my Defender powers would have no effect on my elf abilities. I thought of Grandmother, directing my powers at her, and she appeared. I knew, of course, that only I could see the portal. I waved to

Grandmother, and the two boys stared at where the portal was. They glanced at each other and rolled their eyes. I picked up an empty plastic cup and asked, "Are you watching?"

"Yes, Miss Defender," Ray said sarcastically.

Are you OK? Grandmother asked.

Yes, I think these boys will help but they don't believe me. Will you catch this and throw it back?

Yes, dear.

I made sure the boys were watching and tossed the cup through. There was a slight delay, then it appeared on Grandmother's side and she caught it. But to the boys, the cup simply vanished.

Ray ran to where the cup disappeared, looking every which way. "What kind of trick is this?"

"No trick. My grandmother's staring back at you." She waved, though I'm not sure why since he couldn't see her. I let my portal vanish. She made a new one, since portals are one-way, and appeared holding the cup.

Tell him to get ready, she said.

Oh, I will, I said, smiling. *Watch out, Ray,* I said in my head, hoping it wouldn't register with Grandmother that

I was speaking telepathically and not out loud to him. She tossed the cup. Ray didn't move. And it bopped him right on the nose. "Ow!"

Grandmother winced. *Carol, dear, that wasn't nice.* But she was trying not to laugh. Ray rubbed his nose and Ivan-I-Am-Not stared at me wide-eyed. "How did you do that?"

"Elves can make portals. I'm part elf. Actually, I could jump through a portal right now and there'd be nothing you could do about it." Ray lurched forward as if he might try to stop me. "But I won't," I said. "I'm hoping you can help us."

"Why should we help you?"

"Because I can bring back Santa."

The boys looked at each other and seemed to speak without saying anything. "OK, we'll hear you out," Ray finally said.

"Thank you." *I trust them,* I said to Grandmother. She nodded and dove through the portal. Both boys jumped back when the elf materialized in front of them. Ivan-I-Am-Not shrieked and fled to the other side of the station. "It's OK," I said. "This is my grandmother. She's called the Ancient One."

Ray studied my grandmother, almost as if he were looking at a sculpture in a museum. He started to touch her face and Grandmother swatted his hand away.

"Ouch!" Ray yelled, and I stifled a giggle.

"What's the idea of kidnapping my granddaughter, young man?" she asked, putting her hands on her hips.

"I-I-I," Ray stuttered.

"I-I-I, what?" she snapped.

"We did it to protect her."

"What do you mean?" I asked.

"If they found you first, that would be it. They'd either eliminate you or make you one of them."

"Who?"

"The White Stripes," Ray said, exasperated. "The ones who rule. Don't you know anything?"

"I told you I'm not from here," I said.

"Carol, dear, I have an idea if our new friend is willing. Remember how I told you my story through The Sharing?" she asked. "Well, elves can also draw out others' stories. That would be a good way to learn about this young man and his world. It takes two of us, though. You'll have to help."

"But I don't know how."

"It's not hard, that is, if our friend isn't too scared to do it." She flashed a devilish grin at me.

Ray puffed out his chest like a cartoon rooster. "I'm not scared."

"Good," Grandmother said. "No time to waste." She grabbed his hand, then mine, and before I knew what was happening, a jolt of what felt like electricity coursed through us. My brain filled with a jumble of images: of Grandmother as a young elf, then an old elf, then the boy as a baby, as a toddler, then a teenager, pieces of their lives zipping around my brain. I heard Grandmother's voice. *Focus on his memories, Carol. Pull them toward you.* I concentrated on the images of Ray, trying to make them my own. My head ached, sort of like when you eat ice cream too fast. But I could feel it working. There was a flash of light and just as I'd watched the history of my grandmother a year earlier, I watched Ray's life unfold. I witnessed what could only be called a tragedy.

CHAPTER 3

The Supreme Leader

I see a little boy with bright red hair and he's on a playground in the falling snow. A hundred kids scurry and scream around him. But not the boy. He's five, in kindergarten I somehow know, and he's lying on his back watching the snow fall, feeling it land on his face, the flakes tickling the tip of his nose and making him feel like he has to sneeze. He wants to make a snow angel, as his mom told him they would after the first big snow, but there's not enough on the ground yet.

They haven't been here long, in this little town on Long Island called Central Islip, but he likes his school and he likes his teacher, the pretty lady with blonde hair. He catches his parents staring at his red hair sometimes and looking puzzled, even worried. But his mother calls it "a gift from God, His way of showing you're unique." A few children tease him, but the teacher puts a stop to that. Most of the kids are nice and he's made lots of friends who sometimes come to his house after school to play.

The boy opens his mouth, wondering what snowflakes taste like, or if they have any taste at all. He remembers they're made of water, though he's still not quite sure how frozen water winds up in the sky. He sticks out his tongue and watches the flakes fall. The biggest flake ever, round as the $1 Glover coin he got for his birthday, floats right for him. He moves his head a bit and sticks his tongue out as far as it can go, and when the flake lands on the tip, the world explodes in white. He feels electrified, like that day his mom took him to the children's museum and he touched the metal ball that shoots sparks and makes your hair stand on end. The snowflake doesn't hurt exactly, but he leaps off the ground and screams at the shock of it. All the children stop and look, the playground falling silent.

He notices the stares first, then his hat lying in the snow, the teacher rushing over to find out if he's OK. When she sees him, she gasps, and her rosy cheeks turn as white as the falling snow. She grabs his hat, yanks it back over his head, and roughly leads him by the hand to the principal's office. She makes a call and his mother arrives a few minutes later, out of breath, not even wearing her gray uniform, just the sweatshirt and jogging pants she always has on around the house. She and the teacher whisper and steal glances his way, and his mom grabs him by the hand and they hurry out the door. "Am I in trouble, Mommy?"

"Shhh," she says. "Not now. We need to call your father."

Once they are home, his father shows up and his parents huddle in the kitchen while he plays half-heartedly in the living room, terrified by the cloud of fear that seems to have settled on his house. The next thing he knows, his parents are stuffing clothes in suitcases and his mom is telling him to grab his favorite toy. "Only one." So he chooses his Glover's Raiders Commando Doll. His mom winces but tosses it into a suitcase. His dad is already loading the other suitcases into the minivan, along with food and water and soap and shampoo. His mom hurries him out the door and straps him into the car seat. She glances at his hair, then the house, and tears spill down her cheeks. "What's happening, Mommy? Are we going on a trip?"

"Yes, *Papi*. To see friends."

"Who?"

"You'll see when we get there." She pulls a hat onto his head, down around the ears, even though the minivan is toasty and warm. His father is behind the wheel, the engine running, the windshield wipers slapping away the driving snow. "Hurry, Lidia."

His mother jumps in and slams the door. She looks in the side mirror and lets out a yelp. The boy turns to see a black car pulling in behind them, blocking the driveway. "How did they find out?" his mother asks.

"The teacher," his father says.

"She wouldn't do that."

"She would to protect herself. Can you blame her?" His father looks hard at his mother. "If I tell you to go, you go."

"I won't leave you."

"You have to." He glances at his son and whispers, "They'll take him." The boy's mother nods. A man gets out of the black car. He's wearing a black suit with a white shirt and black tie. The boy has never seen a man in a suit before, except on TV. The man approaches the driver's side.

"I love you, OK?" the father says, touching the boy's cheek.

"OK, Daddy."

"Do you love me?"

"Yes, Daddy."

"Good." He turns to his wife. "Remember, run." Then he gets out of the van. His mother slides into the driver's seat and watches her husband talk with the man in black. The chat appears friendly at first. He hears the man ask, muffled, "Where you heading?"

"See some family," the father answers.

"School day, isn't it?" the man asks, trying to look in the window of the van.

His father steps to block his view. "How do you know we have a child? Why is it any of your business where we go? Who are you?"

The man stares at the father and says coldly, "You know who I am."

There's a long, tense silence. Then the father yells, "Go!" and he tackles the man around the waist. The two of them land in the front yard in the deepening snow. The boy's mother throws the van into reverse and jams her foot on the gas. The van slams into the idling black car blocking the driveway, sliding across the snowy road toward the Robinsons' house. The boy screams. His mother tries to take off. But the black car, tilted from the impact, is stuck on the back of the van. His mother slams the steering wheel. She's crying, her panic infecting the boy. He screams.

His father and the man wrestle in the front yard. Then his dad lies still, and the man gets up, brushing snow from his black suit. He turns to look at them and smiles. It is the most awful smile the boy has ever seen. The man walks toward them. His mother mutters, "No, no, no, no." She presses her foot on the gas and the van lurches. But the black car holds them back.

The man yells, "Get out of the vehicle!" He's no longer smiling.

"No," his mother screams. "You can't have him."

"We won't hurt him. He's a White Stripe. He's important."

The boy's panic grows and grows. His mother screams again. "Never!" And her fury, like her panic, washes over the boy. He screams again with all his might. He feels as if he might explode. And then he does. Or it seems that way. The doors of the van blow open. The back hatch flies up. The black car skids across the street. The man, standing next to the van, is struck by the passenger door and is launched backward into the yard. He lands with a dull thud and hits his head on the snowy, frozen ground. He lies still. His mother flies forward but the force of the explosion pops the air bag, saving her from bouncing her face off the steering wheel. Her nose is bleeding, she appears woozy, but she shakes her head, trying to regain her senses. The man on the ground stirs. The boy's mom looks back at her son with eyes wide. She jams her foot on the gas. The man pulls himself to his feet and watches them vanish. They never return to their home in Central Islip. The boy never sees his school or his friends or the pretty blonde teacher again. And the vision of his father, lying motionless in the deepening snow, is the last one he ever has of him.

For the longest time, the boy's mom shields him from whatever danger they face, through their years on the run, bouncing from friend to friend. She works as a hairdresser wherever she can, home-schooling him as best she's able.

"Why can't I go to a real school?" he asks, and she always dodges the question with an "I'll tell you when you're old enough." He wonders when that day will come, but he begins to figure things out for himself. His mom won't let him go online unless she's around and then mostly for the school lessons she's pieced together from educational sites. She's smart, he knows that, but she went no further than high school and a couple of years in beauty school. "We'll study together," she says. "There are a million ways to learn."

He doesn't argue, and he loves to read and he aces the tests she devises. But what he truly wants to learn is why they live the way they do, why he has to spend most of his time in whatever tiny apartment they call home, escaping only to go to a park for early-morning exercise, or to eat at a restaurant on a special occasion. And he wonders why his mom dyes his hair black once a month, covering up the red hair and the white stripe.

He wants to search those very words online—"red hair/white stripe"—if he could ever get time alone with the computer and figure out her password. Shortly after he turns eleven, he finally decides the time has come. She's at her hairdressing job, not due home for two hours, so he pulls the laptop from the back of the closet where she thinks it's safely hidden. He feels as though he might burst with the excitement of rebellion. He flips the computer on, and after a bunch of tries with password combinations, it occurs to him: his birthday and hers. On the fourth attempt, he is in.

When the screen lights up with the Internet home page, he feels a thrill. And he feels guilt. This is the first time he has ever defied his mother on such a scale. Sure, he talks back once in a while or pouts when he doesn't get his way. But this is different. This is something she's made him promise to never do.

"I know you have questions, *mi'jo*," his mother says. "And I'll answer them when the time is right."

"When will that be?" he asks. "I'm big now. I want to know what's going on."

"Soon," she promises.

But soon isn't soon enough. He is sick of waiting, sick of feeling like the rest of the world is in on something he isn't. He clicks on the glover.com search engine, recognizing the face of the world's Supreme Leader at the top of the home page. He knows a little about him from the occasional newspaper he sneaks a peek at and a newscast or radio report he overhears, but the Supreme Leader is another subject that's off-limits with his mother. "I do not want that name uttered in this house."

"Why?"

"When you're older, Ray."

"That's not fair!"

"Life's not fair," his mother says. "Listen to me, Ray. If anyone ever comes for us, just run. Don't worry about me. I can take care of myself."

"I won't leave you, Mommy."

"Oh, *mi'jo*, you have to," she says. "You're special, don't you know that? And bad people in this world covet special things. I would die if they got you."

"But who, Mommy?"

"Never mind that. It's for your own protection. I'll explain some day."

But she never has. He suspects it has something to do with the Supreme Leader, and now that he has the password, he'll research what he can find on him. But later. For the moment, he has more pressing matters. He types in his search terms. Hunting and pecking the keys. His mom can homeschool him, but she sure can't teach him to type. "Red hair/white stripe," he enters and hits return.

What he finds makes the hairs on his arms stand on end. They call it "The Mark," his white stripe, and it means he is indeed special, but not for the reasons his mother has given him. Nothing to do with showing his uniqueness, though apparently, he is one of only a few with The Mark, including the one who rules them all.

He is surprised to see the image of the Supreme Leader pop up. What does he have to do with red hair with a white stripe? He clicks on a button that says, "The Supreme Leader welcomes you," and is taken to another surprising image, a photograph of the Supreme Leader at the head of a large oval table surrounded by men and women, all of whom have red hair with a white stripe. A narrator's voice comes through the speaker of his mother's computer, so loudly that it startles him.

"The White Stripe Council holds an exalted place in society, relied upon by our Supreme Leader to provide wisdom in dealing with this sometimes troubled world. No one knows where The Mark comes from, but its bearer offers abilities that only the Supreme Leader has been able to harness for the greater good. So if you have The Mark, do not fear. It is a great gift. Join us. Work by our side on the White Stripe Council. And if you know someone who has The Mark, give him the good news that he is special. And if he does not understand, contact us immediately and we will do all we can to bring this special person into the fold. The Supreme Leader wants you. The Supreme Leader needs you. The Supreme Leader loves you."

The boy sits back with a thud. His mind churns. So, he is special? It's amazing to contemplate the idea that the Supreme Leader, the man who rules the entire world, could need *his* help. Probably only when he is older, naturally, but still. He suddenly feels important, instead of like a freak to be hidden away.

Has his mother heard of the White Stripe Council? What does she know that he doesn't? And how will he even ask her? To start raising questions will give away the fact that he's defied her. He studies the button at the bottom of the page that reads, "If you know someone with

The Mark, click to learn more." He thinks about it, takes a deep breath, and clicks.

Up comes a screen with another picture of the Supreme Leader, this time smiling, his arms open as if to welcome the boy. But before he can explore further, his computer dings. A white pop-up box with red borders appears. He watches as letter after letter materializes inside the box, as if someone is typing at that very moment.

THEY ARE COMING.

His stomach drops. He looks around. Maybe his mother has set this up to scare him. But no, she isn't capable of something like that. The cursor under the message flashes and he realizes he can type a response.

"Who?" he asks.

GO TO PARK AT BLOCK'S END. 15 MINUTES. TOPS.

"Who are you?" he types.

NO TIME. ARE FRIENDS. WE'VE BEEN WATCHING. GO NOW OR DEARLY PAY.

The box vanishes, and he sits alone in the tiny apartment, thinking, wondering if someone is playing a practical joke on him. But what if the mysterious message is right? Something about the web page nags at him, especially the part where it urges people to tell the government if they know someone with The Mark. That sounds an awful lot like turning someone in. What if the nosy old lady down the hall spotted his red and white hair and decided to let the government know? How would he like that? He looks at his watch. Five minutes have passed. He's running out of time. He has ten minutes. Tops.

He closes the page and flips off the computer, stashing it back in the closet. He puts on his uniform. He grabs his key and the hat his mother makes him wear on the rare occasions she allows him to leave the apartment. "Just in case," she says, covering his close-cropped dyed hair. He grabs a bottle of water—it is August in New York, the pavement smoldering—and peeks out the door of the apartment, making sure the nosy old lady isn't watching. The last thing he needs is her tattling to his mother. He isn't supposed to go out by himself, though sometimes he sneaks to the corner store for a pack of gum.

He edges down the hall to the top of the stairs. They live on the fourth floor, but he avoids the rickety elevator because who knows who might be standing there when the doors open. THEY might be waiting. Down the stairs he goes, two at a time. He pauses in the lobby, which is empty midafternoon, most of the building's residents at work or in their apartments with their ACs cranked up. He continues to the entrance where he pauses again to assess the street. Washington Heights is a beehive of activity, filled with mostly Dominicans and other Latinos, along with a few young white people seeking affordable rents. His mother is Dominican so when she decided to leave Long Island to run from whatever they were running from, Washington Heights seemed as good a place as any. "It's easy to get lost in a city of eight million," she says. "We'd stick out like a sore brown thumb in the country." Not knowing why they were running in the first place, he never argued. And he likes the city and its crazy energy, the pulsing merengue and bachata in the neighboring apartments, the bodegas where you can buy empanadas, the old Dominican ladies wheeling their carts filled with groceries—always with plantains and avocados and yucca.

He scans the street for anything out of the ordinary and hurries toward the end of the block. He crosses the street to the tiny green space where young mothers watch their children climb the monkey bars, or push them in their tiny swings. He finds a tree to lean on that provides both shade and a clear view of his block. One of the mothers eyes him suspiciously. He smiles at her, but she glances at her child as if to warn him to stay clear.

He waits, taking sips of his water, the seconds crawling by. And then, from the other end of the block, turning off Broadway, two long black cars, sparkling in the August sun, roar down 175th Street. These aren't the beat-up black sedans of the gypsy cab drivers. They are shiny black, with tinted windows and glistening silver hubcaps. The cars stop in front of his building and from each vehicle emerge two men, dressed head to toe in dark suits, sunglasses shielding their eyes. They look up and down the block. One gazes directly at Ray, and even though he is several hundred feet away, shrouded by the shade of the park tree, it feels as though the man sees him, gazing right into his soul. A chill brushes his spine and he shrinks farther into shadow. Three of the men disappear into his building. The fourth waits by the car.

That's when he spots her. His mother. Hurrying around the corner of the block. What is she doing home?

Her shift doesn't end for two hours. The shop is only a few blocks away; had someone called her? The nosy old lady? Then he remembers. The computer, her cell phone, it's all on the same account. She must have been alerted that someone had logged in. And that someone, she surely knew, was him. She stops at the corner when she spots the black cars. She hesitates and he wonders if she'll run. No, she would never leave him. She walks toward the building, head down, trying not to be noticed by the man in black. He's turned the other direction, and Ray thinks for just a moment that his mom will make it past. But the man turns as she heads up the front steps to their building.

The man notices her and takes off. He doesn't even hesitate, as if he knows who she is. He grabs her by the arm and pulls her down the steps. Ray drops his bottle of water and starts forward. He has to protect her. The man drags her to the car. She takes a swing at him, but his mother is tiny and the man grabs her wrist as he would a child's. He tosses her into the back of the second black car. Ray is running now. He starts to shout but thinks better of it. He needs to surprise the man in black, knock him to the sidewalk, open the door, and make a break for it with his mom. He'll promise to listen from now on, to never, ever defy her again.

He crosses the street, against the light, dodging honking cabs, running as hard as he can. The moment his foot hits the sidewalk, there is a blur from his right, someone moving fast. And that someone's shoulder is in his gut and he's lifted off his feet and forced up the sidewalk out of view of the man in black.

"Hey," he starts to shout, but it comes out "Hehhhhh . . . ." as the air is knocked out of him. The two of them hit the sidewalk. His elbows scrape painfully on the cement.

"It's too late!" Ray looks up in surprise at who has tackled him. A boy, about his age. "Nothing can be done."

Ray pushes him off. The boy is skinny to the point of looking starved. His uniform is dirty. He has brown hair but with traces of red. "Let me go!" Ray shouts and jumps to his feet. The man's still guarding the car in which his mother has been put. The other men emerge from the building. They look up and down the street. As their eyes swing in his direction, the boy pulls him to the ground.

"Do not be foolish," he hisses. "We must run."

"I can't leave her," Ray says. He is crying. "It's my fault they came."

"It does not matter," the boy says. "They always come." The boy pulls him away, half-dragging him across the sidewalk. From the ground, Ray sees the legs of the dark-suited men spreading out, going up and down the street. Searching. For him.

Ray thinks back to what his mom always told him. "If anyone ever comes for us, just run." These are the bad people she'd feared. And though it rips out his insides to leave her, he knows he has to do as she told him. He makes a promise to himself that he will come back for her one day. He will save her. But not today. Today, he will obey her and run.

He and the boy slink along the sidewalk, ducking behind parked cars on the crowded Washington Heights street. Passersby look at them strangely. One in particular glances from him and the boy and back to where the men advance. Ray sees something in the man's eyes. "Please, no," Ray says to the man. But the man smiles, a nasty grin, and he shouts, "They're here! Over here!"

The boy takes off, dragging Ray with him. The man shouts even louder. "They're here! They're here! I want my reward." Ray and the boy round the corner. Ray hears one of the men ask the traitor, "Which way?"

"Only if I get my reward."

"You'll get something all right. Tell us where!"

"That way."

Ray and the boy dodge people on the street. A police officer eyes them suspiciously as they zip past. "Stop them!" comes a shout from up the block. The officer joins the chase.

"This way," the boy says, and he makes an abrupt turn into the entrance of a subway station. Down the stairs they fly. Ray takes the last four in one leap, stumbling at the bottom. They sprint through the station. Ray bumps a man with a briefcase and it pops open, papers flying, the man letting loose a string of curses.

The boy leaps over the turnstile, Ray at his heels. A transit worker shouts, "Hey!" Ray glances back and sees the police officer and the transit worker climbing over the turnstiles, the men in black right behind them.

They run down the platform. A train is pulling into the station and the boy shouts, "No!" The train slows to a stop and the doors bang open.

"We're not getting on?" Ray asks. They push through the crowds toward the end of the station.

"No."

"Where are we going?"

The doors close, and the train starts to pull out of the station. Ray begins to feel strange. Everything seems to slow down. "Fight it!" the boy says. The train has come to a stop again, making no sound. All the passengers who had disembarked are frozen on the platform. He and the boy are the only two moving at all, but they barely can. It's as if they are running underwater, the air around them thick and soupy.

"What's happening?" he asks, trying to shout. His mouth will hardly move.

The boy turns to face their pursuers. Ray fights through the soup to turn with the boy. There is no police officer now, no transit worker. Just the three men in black, charging down the platform. The men get within about twenty feet and stop, which strikes Ray as curious. Why don't they just grab them? "We must try our powers," the boy says, grunting out each word.

"I don't understand," Ray responds. But something tickles at his memory, an image from long ago. A man dressed like these men, stopping them in front of their home. His mother's terror. His father lying in the snowy yard as the evil man approaches. Then his fear and rage and the explosion that came from within. He remembers that and he thinks of his mother being thrown into the back of the car and the men swarming like cockroaches looking for him. And his rage grows.

He steps forward, the soupy air parting before him. He stands shoulder to shoulder with the boy. "Keep away from us!" he shouts, and the men laugh. One of them holds a peculiar-looking machine. Another draws back his hand as if to throw something. He flings his hand forward. The tiny boy does the same. But whatever the man hurls is stronger and it knocks Ray and the boy back. It feels like he's been punched in the nose. Blood trickles to his lip. The fury explodes within him. He leaps to his feet. The boy shakes his head trying to clear it. Ray steps toward the approaching men. He doesn't understand what is happening, but he trembles with power. He draws back his hands like the men did, as if he knows exactly what to do. He flings whatever is within him at the men and it's as if an invisible truck smacks them. Backward they fly, tumbling head over heels down the platform, the machine shattering on the concrete. The train starts moving again. The passengers unfreeze. People scream when they see the men crumpled on the platform. Some run. Others huddle around the men and call for help.

"Holey moley," the boy says beside him. He's gotten to his feet as the chaos erupts and he stares at Ray with eyes wide. The police officer who had been chasing them appears but is distracted by the downed men. "We must go," the boy hisses, and he turns and runs to the edge of the platform. He looks back and motions for Ray to follow. Then he jumps onto the track.

Ray hesitates for just a moment. He glances back at the men. The officer spots him and rises to give chase. Ray sprints to the edge of the platform, jumps down, and follows the mystery boy into the dark bowels of Manhattan. His mother, and life as he knew it, are gone.

Chapter 4

Gallahad

Ray and I emerged from the Sharing just long enough for me to say, "I'm so sorry," before we passed out. And when I awoke, the boys were still asleep but Grandmother was alert.

Are you OK, my sweet?

Yes, Grandmother. My head ached as Ray's memories came back in a rush. *Did you see who the Supreme Leader is?*

Grandmother sighed. *Yes, dearest.*

So he did all this? He changed everything and now rules the whole world?

It appears so.

We need to go back right now and undo it. Let's find the elf while they're sleeping. Ray was sprawled on the floor where he'd collapsed. A blanket had been placed over him, a pillow tucked under his head. Ivan-I-Am-Not was draped across a broken-down recliner next to Ray. He snored softly.

We need to learn more first, Carol. We need to know what your uncle did so we can properly undo it. Or else things could change in even worse ways.

How can things be worse? His mom was kidnapped right in front of him!

I saw, dear. That's why we must find out more. We also need help navigating the city to get to the elf.

Just open a portal to him.

He'll vanish the moment he sees me.

He knows you?

Of course, dear. I'm the one who had him banished.

I groaned. How in the world were we going to get help from an elf with a grudge?

Ray stirred and bolted upright. He moaned and held the side of his head. "I feel like I've been beaten." Ivan-I-Am-Not awoke and rubbed his eyes, which widened at the sight of us, as if maybe he thought he'd dreamed our arrival. I wondered what he'd done during the Sharing.

Ray's eyes were moist and I felt guilty. We had forced

him to relive the worst moments of his life. I wanted to give him a hug. I wanted to tell him things were going to be all right. But that certainly wasn't true, at least not any time soon. We needed to find that elf first. And then I would have to defeat my uncle. Again. And if he had figured out how to change history itself, perhaps he'd grown so powerful I would no longer be a match for him.

"You'll feel better soon," Grandmother said to Ray.

"Do you have anything to eat?" I asked. My stomach rumbled and I felt lightheaded.

Ivan-I-Am-Not crossed over to a small cupboard and took out a loaf of bread, a jar of peanut butter, and a can of green beans. He slathered some peanut butter on the bread and dumped the beans into two beat-up metal bowls. "Here you go," he said.

I grimaced but was so hungry I scarfed the food down anyway. Grandmother ate daintily.

"Are you two on your own?" I asked. They were rail thin. No wonder, if that was all they had to eat.

The boys hesitated, looking at each other before Ray answered. "Our leader disappeared a few days ago. We think he was taken by the White Stripes."

"An adult?" Grandmother asked.

Ray nodded.

"What's his name?" I asked. I thought of my father or Mr. Winters or any of the other Defenders who might exist in this world. Perhaps even Ramon. Maybe he didn't die in this reality. If the Defenders were never formed, we would not have lost him during our mission to save Dad in the Dominican Republic. The mission never would have happened. It was all so confusing.

"He goes by Gallahad," Ray answered. "We don't know his real name, but he's kind of a genius. He messed with their machine so it not only stops the people with power but also detects them. Gallahad wants to find people like us before they do. That's how we found you."

Something tickled my memory. Why did that name sound familiar? But I knew no Gallahad. "I thought maybe it was someone we knew." Then something occurred to me. Why hadn't I thought of it earlier? "Hold on," I said excitedly. "Grandmother, I can make a portal to anyone I know. We can find Dad. Or Mr. Winters."

"But what if your dad works for the Supreme Leader?" Ray asked.

I put my hands on my hips. "Dad would never do that!" I shouted. "Take it back right now!"

"OK, OK," Ray said. "I'm sorry. I take it back." I scowled at him anyway.

"I don't think a portal will work, dear," Grandmother said.

"Why not?"

"Because you don't *know* these versions of your father and Mr. Winters. And they won't know you. So there's no connection."

My very own father wouldn't know me? That was nearly as terrible as losing him altogether. "But you said you could make a portal to the bad elf. How's that possible?"

"Because we live so long, dear. We existed and knew each other before your uncle changed everything."

That made sense, but I still wanted to try. I concentrated on Dad's face, his goofy smile, him calling me Angel Butt. I summoned every ounce of power I could. The portal shimmered, but no one appeared. It was a window to nowhere. I did the same for Mr. Winters. Nothing. Grandmother shook her head. "I'm sorry, dear. They may very well be here, but not as you know them."

I tried hard not to cry. "What do we do then?"

Grandmother turned to the boys. "We need your help getting to the elf."

"You know where he is?" Ray asked.

"The disturbance emanated from the lower part of the city," Grandmother said. "I know exactly where that is. He's lived there since he was exiled. We were almost neighbors. I used to keep my eye on him to make sure he didn't cause trouble, but that was nearly two hundred years ago."

Ivan laughed. Ray sniffed, "Right."

I glared at them. "You don't believe her?"

"You're telling me she's been alive for two hundred years?" Ray asked.

"More like five hundred, young man," Grandmother said evenly.

Ray rolled his eyes.

"Oh, so you just saw an elf appear out of thin air," I said, "but you're not willing to believe she can live for hundreds of years?"

"It doesn't matter what they believe, dear, as long as they help us." Grandmother turned to the boys again. "You *will* help us, right?"

Ray sighed. "Show me where."

Grandmother shuffled across the platform and stopped in front of a huge subway map on the wall, one that showed all of Manhattan and the surrounding boroughs. Someone had drawn on the map, making notes, as a general might when drawing up a battle plan. The lower part of Manhattan was divided from the rest of the city with a thick red line, below which was written "Forbidden Zone." A star with "we are here" sat over 34th Street, west of where I knew Macy's stood. Or used to stand. I wondered if the store existed in this world. If there was no Santa, there'd be no *Miracle on 34th Street*, my favorite movie. No Santa Land on the eighth floor of Macy's. No kids waiting to sit on the Big Guy's lap. So much magic gone from the world.

Grandmother put her finger on the star and traced it past the red line, deep into the Forbidden Zone. "Here," she said.

Ray gasped. "We can't go there."

"Why not?" I asked.

"That's the Supreme Leader's territory."

"He owns that whole part of the city?" I asked.

69

"It's where his government is and the White Stripes all live."

"And where they take prisoners," Ivan-I-Am-Not whispered. "Men in black constantly looking for enemies. For us."

"That's where we need to go," Grandmother said sternly. "There has to be a way."

The boys shook their heads no, but I caught them exchanging a quick glance.

"You know how, don't you?" I asked.

Ray dropped his chin to his chest and sighed. But he pointed to the thick line. "We can't go through." He looked back toward the subway tunnel. "But we can go under. They closed off the subways to the Forbidden Zone for security reasons. One train in, one train out. But there are tunnels and old stations they don't know about." He motioned around us. "Like this one."

"OK, then," I said. "Let's go."

Ray hesitated. "We've only gone so far. There are rumors about monsters. Ones like us who refused to serve the Supreme Leader were forced underground and live in darkness, eating rats and whatever else they can find. It transformed them into something that's not . . . human."

A chill crept along my spine, like a rat skittering across a subway rail. I thought again of my father. He would never submit to someone as evil as his brother. Maybe he had been forced to hide. Maybe he was now a monster. I shuddered at the image of him chasing rats through the tunnels.

"Rubbish," Grandmother said. "Probably rumors this *Supreme Leader* started himself to keep people out of his territory. We go tonight, midnight. If you're too frightened of imaginary monsters to lead the way, Carol and I will figure it out ourselves."

Ray looked hurt. Ivan-I-Am-Not lifted his chin like a soldier posing for a heroic portrait. "I will be going. No monsters scare me." Ray glared at his goofy comrade. But he nodded.

"Good," Grandmother said. "I knew you were brave boys." She hesitated. "I'm sorry, brave young *men*."

Ivan-I-Am-Not struck an even more heroic pose. I tried hard not to smile. Boys sure were simple creatures, easily manipulated. I didn't care what we had to do to get them to help us. I was just happy we had allies. It felt good to finally be doing something. At last, we had a mission.

I'd never seen such darkness. Though I guess *seen* is the wrong word, because we couldn't *see* anything. Only blackness as we walked deep into the abandoned subway tunnel. Before we started out, Ray told us it was best not to use any light until we absolutely had to. "Just to be safe." We didn't want to draw the attention of any "monsters" in the tunnels. And a trickle of light might escape through a manhole and alert the Supreme Leader's men to our presence.

No one else would be out on the streets at midnight because of the strict 10 p.m. curfew. If you were caught without proper papers, you'd be arrested, or simply vanish. "It's a police state," Grandmother muttered.

We walked without a word, Ray leading the way and Ivan-I-Am-Not bringing up the rear. The silence was as deep and thick as the blackness, except for the sounds of our footsteps and the occasional scurrying of some unseen creature. I was wearing a gray uniform Ray had scrounged up, a small attempt to blend into this strange world. The Ancient One, notoriously stubborn, refused to wear the clothes he offered her.

We walked for a good half hour. I would touch Grandmother's shoulder, and she would squeeze my hand and I'd feel less frightened. At long last, Ray flipped on his flashlight. Ivan-I-Am-Not did the same. The narrow focus of the beams revealed little of our surroundings, but debris was scattered along the edges of the tracks. I saw a flash of movement, and a tail, a rat vanishing to parts unknown. Water dripped from above, making a puddle in front of us.

"This is as far as we've come," Ray said. "Gallahad didn't want us to risk going any farther. We're at the edge of the Forbidden Zone. He was headed this way when he vanished."

"Why was he coming here?" I asked.

"Reconnaissance," Grandmother answered for them. "Know the enemy in order to defeat him."

"Yes, looking for weaknesses," Ray said. "But we're afraid he got captured."

"Or monsters grab him," Ivan-I-Am-Not whispered.

"Are you sure you want to do this?" Ray asked.

"Do you like this world?" I responded. "Do you like hiding underground?" The boys said nothing. "Then let me fix it. I know I can." I said the words with as much conviction as I could muster, trying to convince them— and maybe me.

Ray headed deeper into the tunnel, the flashlight dancing along the dripping walls and debris-strewn track. Our footsteps seemed to echo more loudly the farther we went into the Forbidden Zone. I could hear my own heart, like a bass drum in my chest. Grandmother's breathing grew heavier. When Ray kicked a piece of rusty metal, the clanging was so loud I thought the entire world would hear us. Ivan-I-Am-Not yelped and we all froze. But nothing appeared. No men in black. No monsters.

A few minutes later, however, I felt it. A presence. Someone, or *something*, was watching us. *We're not alone, dear*, Grandmother said telepathically.

I know. My heart beat so loud, I imagined the pounding had revealed us to whoever was watching. *Should we go back?*

No. We'll just have to deal with it. Get a pulse ready.

But won't they detect my use of Defender power?

We may not have a choice.

I moved my hand around, gathering up a powerful North Pulse, ready to fling it at what lay beyond the shadows. Suddenly Ivan-I-Am-Not hissed, "A monster!" Glowing red eyes, horrible and pulsing, moved toward us. I drew back my hand. More red eyes appeared. This was going to be a fight. The voice stopped me.

"No, m'lady!"

I nearly cried out at the sound of it. Joy overwhelmed me. I let go of the web, searching wildly for the source of the voice. No one else would use those words. It had to be him. "Mr. Winters?" I called out.

There was a long silence. The red eyes stared out at us. Ivan-I-Am-Not whimpered. Ray squatted as if ready to leap in attack. Grandmother tried to catch her breath. At last, the voice answered. "How do you know that name?" A man stepped from the shadows. Others did the same. They all wore contraptions that had two glowing red lights on the front. Night-vision goggles. The man removed his.

Ray gasped. "Gallahad!"

I gasped, too. "Mr. Winters!" And I sprinted toward him, ready to throw my arms around him. But he stepped back.

"Carol, no!" Grandmother shouted, and I stopped.

"Mr. Winters, it's me," I said. "It's Carol."

Gallahad stared at me blankly. He looked pretty much the same, with his striped red hair cut short. Only he was thinner, wiry looking. "I don't know any Carol," he said. "How do you know my name? Are you a spy?"

It was all I could do to keep from crying. I'd finally found someone I knew in this world, and he didn't even recognize me. "But you do know me," I said softly, trying to make it so.

"Carol, dear, he doesn't. Not here."

"What are they talking about?" Mr. Winters asked Ray. "And why are you in the Forbidden Zone?"

"It's hard to explain," Ray answered. "She's OK. They're both OK." He looked around at the glowing goggle eyes. They gave me the creeps. "Who are these people? Where have you been, Gallahad?"

Suddenly I remembered. Gallahad! One of King Arthur's Knights of the Roundtable. That's how the Mr. Winters I knew viewed the Defenders, as knights willing to lay down their lives to protect Santa. It's why he'd gotten into the habit of calling everyone "m'lady" or "m'lord." The same sort of thinking must have led this Mr. Winters to adopt the nickname Gallahad. That made me smile.

"I've been recruiting allies," he answered, pointing to the red eyes that surrounded us. "Brothers and sisters in arms." His face had softened. He looked more like the Mr. Winters I had known. My heart ached for him to remember me.

"They're allies, too," Ray said, pointing to me and Grandmother. "They say they can change things."

Mr. Winters studied us. "And you trust them?"

"You trust them?" Ray asked, pointing to the red eyes.

Mr. Winters nodded. "Follow us."

After another twenty minutes of walking, a light appeared down the track. The people in the goggles took them off, and I could finally see their faces. Men and women. Young and old. A few teenagers. Two of them—an older man and a young woman—had the red hair with the white stripe. I was hoping I'd recognize more Defenders, but neither looked familiar. They studied me warily.

When we reached the light, we emerged into another abandoned station, and the sight took my breath away.

Aside from the people (there had to be nearly fifty), the only way to describe the station was with a simple word: beautiful. Christmas lights in red, green, white, and purple covered the walls, the old turnstiles, and the ticket booth. Tinsel was draped everywhere and glittered in the soft light. And in the center of it all stood a tree, beautifully decorated with a mix of carved wooden ornaments, more twinkling lights, strings of popcorn, silver icicles, and a shimmering star on top. Beneath the tree were dozens of packages wrapped in newspaper, plain brown paper, or whatever scraps could be found and tied with lovely homemade ribbons and bows. Beside the tree stood something that brought tears to my eyes: a large wooden Santa, meticulously carved, painted in bright white and deep red. Someone was a true artist. Everyone watched in silence as I approached the Santa and touched his face, crying softly for this beautiful symbol of my lost world.

"You know that man?" Mr. Winters asked.

"Santa," I answered, and a murmur spread through the station.

Mr. Winters's eyes widened. "And you've read the book?"

I glanced at Grandmother, who shrugged. "What book?" I asked.

Mr. Winters motioned toward an old man with a long gray beard. A hush fell over the room. The old man took a key from his pocket and knelt to open an ancient trunk. He removed a tattered-looking leather-bound book, lifting it gently, as if it might break into pieces at any sudden movement. From the looks of it, I thought it just might. He handed the book to Mr. Winters, who stepped beside me and turned to the title page. A musty smell tickled my nostrils.

"*A Christmas Carol*," Mr. Winters said, as if he were speaking of a holy book.

"Yes, I know it. Charles Dickens. You were reading it the first time I met you."

Mr. Winters looked at me as if I'd lost my mind. "This book is banned. This is the only copy I've ever seen. We in the Underground have passed around hand-copied versions, but the real books were destroyed long ago."

My mind raced. The book that gave me my nickname, the name I had embraced once I'd discovered my true destiny, that book was forbidden in this awful world.

You know why, Carol, Grandmother said. *Dickens painted a world of magic and generosity and goodness around Christmas. If your uncle wanted to destroy Christmas as we knew it, one of the most beloved books of all time would have to go, too.*

"So, if this book is banned, how do people celebrate Christmas?" I asked.

"All celebrations center around the Supreme Leader," Mr. Winters said. "People buy gifts in his stores. The more you buy, the more favor you gain with him. Those who are rich, get richer and more powerful. And the Supreme Leader is the richest and most powerful of all."

"But what about less fortunate kids?" I looked around. A few young faces, dirty and gaunt, stared back at me. I couldn't believe how skinny they all were. I wondered how they survived in these tunnels. Did they ever see the sun? Or take in deep breaths of fresh air on a crisp winter's morning? Or do something as simple as ride a bike? I would go crazy if I had to live in such a place.

"Parents do what they can," Mr. Winters said. "Some make gifts. To me, that's a purer form of giving because it's from a place of love, not wealth."

I thought of my best friend Amelia, how her parents struggled and she received only a fraction of the gifts I did when I lived with my uncle. Yet, what she received was a gift more priceless than all the gold in the world: a family's love. That's something Uncle Christopher never gave me. "We can fix it," I said.

Mr. Winters laughed. Whispers and chuckles flitted about the room. "A little girl and an old woman?" He motioned at the station and everyone in it. "Will fix all this?" I stared at him in angry disbelief. The man who had told me a girl was capable of anything, who made me believe in myself, who loved me like a daughter, he sounded almost cruel. This world had made him a different man. A bitter man.

"I'll have you know I'm an elf, not a woman," Grandmother snapped. "And this *little girl* defeated your ridiculous Supreme Leader in our world."

Mr. Winters snorted. "What do you want from us?"

"They need to get to someone who lives in the Forbidden Zone," Ray said.

"Where?"

"Close to the palace."

"That's suicide," Mr. Winters said. "I'll have nothing to do with it."

"Please, Mr. Winters," I said, stepping closer to him. I tried not to focus on how different this Mr. Winters was. His gleaming white teeth were dirty and dull from neglect. The sparkle that always seemed to be in his eyes had been extinguished. Like the others, he looked hungry and ragged in his dirty gray uniform. I tried to concentrate on what I knew was within him: goodness, kindness, courage.

But this Mr. Winters turned away from me. He returned the Dickens book to the trunk. "Feel free to get yourself arrested, or worse. You'll have to find help elsewhere." He slammed the trunk shut as an exclamation point.

"What happened to you?" I screamed. "In my world, you are brave and strong and the first person who had faith in me. The Mr. Winters I know isn't a coward."

"Call me all the names you want, little girl. This Mr. Winters doesn't have a death wish."

I crossed my arms and stomped my feet, probably looking like the "little girl" he accused me of being. But I didn't care.

From behind me came a voice so soft I barely heard it. "I'll go." Ray stepped forward. He cleared his throat and repeated himself, louder this time. "I'll go." The room came alive with whispers. Mr. Winters glared at the boy. Ray looked away.

Then Ivan-I-Am-Not stepped up, standing shoulder to shoulder with his friend. "Me also," he said. He wouldn't even make eye contact with Mr. Winters but stole a glance at me. I smiled at him and mouthed the words, "Thank you."

"You'll do no such thing," Mr. Winters said. "We have to be smart. This isn't smart."

"And what are we doing down here, Gallahad?" Ray shouted. "Living like rats, hiding. What's the point?"

"We're gathering strength. Building resistance."

"We are losing," Ivan-I-Am-Not said. "Nothing we do."

Mr. Winters stared at the floor for a long time. An almost unbearable tension seeped through the silence. Someone coughed, making me jump. Finally, Mr. Winters said, "You boys are the only family I have. I can't lose you." There was a hint of the kindness he had shown me in my world. It gave me hope.

"You won't," I said. "I'll protect them."

Mr. Winters stared hard at me and I met his gaze. "How can you be so sure, m'lady?"

My heart ached at those words. In truth, I couldn't be sure. I didn't know what kind of forces I was up against. I might lose. We might die. But I had no choice but to believe I could do it, that we could come together to defeat my uncle and restore the world. "I can't be, Mr. Winters. You know that. But I will do everything in my power to keep us safe. I need your help, though. Will you join us?"

Mr. Winters glanced at Ray and Ivan-I-Am-Not. They moved closer to me. He looked at Grandmother, who winked at him. Everyone in the station leaned in, holding a collective breath.

Mr. Winters's face hardened and the words he spoke once again jabbed me in my fragile heart. "I will not be a part of this madness," he growled. The whole world seemed to deflate. And as he stormed off, my tears came. And they didn't stop for a long time.

CHAPTER 5

Finding the Castle

Elves, I was about to learn, become forgetful when they're old. Just like humans. Though to be fair to Grandmother, it had been close to two hundred years. I'd probably forget, too. We wandered through the tunnels for nearly two hours, the night-vision goggles the "monsters" loaned us giving everything a ghostly green glow. I wondered again if our new allies spent their entire lives wandering around dark tunnels that were eerily illuminated by the goggles. Maybe they always would if I didn't change things.

As I stumbled through the tunnels, my heart hammered again. Every shadow could conceal a man in black. My imagination ran wild with thoughts of giant mutant rats ruling the tunnels. Or other humans, definitely not like our allies, living down here alone, resorting to cannibalism to survive. Perhaps even bitter, twisted elves escaped to the tunnels and would defend what territory they had left. But all we saw were scurrying rats (not the mutant kind), dripping water, and hissing pipes. No one else appeared. And we emerged through a manhole near Jane Street. That's where Grandmother insisted the wayward elf had lived for more than two centuries. "I can see his house like it was yesterday."

Ray had conferred with Ivan-I-Am-Not, studying the map to determine the best place to exit to reach the elf. Mr. Winters never returned. We were on our own. "We need to be on the streets as little as possible," Ray had said. "It'll be a miracle if we're not spotted."

Now the moment had come and, leaving our goggles behind, the four of us slithered out of the manhole and dashed to cover in the shadows. The whole area was quiet and deserted. Streetlights shone but barely penetrated the gloominess, as if the dark force that ruled this world had taken form and enveloped lower Manhattan. I thought of the creeping darkness in *A Wrinkle in Time* and shuddered, trying hard to be as brave as Meg.

Grandmother looked around, then up at the street signs, and said to me telepathically: *Uh-oh.*

What do you mean uh-oh?

I think we're on the wrong block. This doesn't look familiar.

It's probably changed after two hundred years.

Not his house. It was huge, like an old castle. I would recognize it immediately. Hand me the map.

The gray-bearded man had loaned me the small map, and Grandmother unfolded it quietly, studying the maze of streets and buildings. "Oops," she muttered.

"What's wrong?" Ray whispered, glancing up and down the street.

"It's not this part of Jane Street. It's three blocks over." She pointed to a block west of the location she'd highlighted before we left.

"You're kidding," Ray said. Ivan-I-Am-Not slapped his hand to head.

"Let's go back underground," I suggested.

"It doesn't work like that," Ray said, his voice edging above a whisper. We have to follow the subway lines."

I turned to Grandmother. "Can we make a portal to outside the house?"

"The elf will sense it and run."

Ray groaned. "Then we'll have to go on the streets. Keep to the shadows."

We crept along Jane Street, our shuffling feet sounding like a stampede of buffalo in the thick silence. The emptiness made my skin crawl. New York was supposed to be the City That Never Sleeps, the streets teeming with people and endless things to do. But it was as if everyone had been abducted, or a plague had wiped out the population. Ray held up his hand for us to stop and pointed to a camera above a dimly glowing streetlight. The camera rotated toward us and we ducked behind a corner food stand. The camera panned, pausing when it pointed at us. We held our breath. But then it started back the way it had come, and we exhaled in relief. We scampered across the empty street.

As we navigated the maze that was Downtown Manhattan, I saw my uncle. Again and again and again. On ads in bus stops: THE SUPREME LEADER LOVES YOU. On a billboard that towered over a government-looking building: TOGETHER WE WILL BUILD A PROSPEROUS FUTURE. Even on a TV screen that flickered inside a storefront, his floating face seeming to stare right through me.

He took a page right out of Orwell, Grandmother said.

What do you mean?

I haven't made you read 1984 *yet?*

No.

Pity. Your uncle is like Big Brother, this terrible ruler in Orwell's book. The government watches your every move, and if you speak out against them, you're a traitor.

That's horrible.

Yes, dear. When we undo all of this, you need to read the book.

I appreciated the fact that Grandmother said "when," not "if," but looking around at the world my uncle had created, it was hard to believe we could undo so much damage.

Ahead of us, Ray raised his hand again, pointing above. Another camera. Thank goodness he was with us. I never would have spotted it. We would have been captured already, or in a fight for our lives, men in black aiming their power-nullifying machines at us. We waited in the shadows for the camera to pan past and then sprinted across the street. "One more block," Ray whispered, and I felt a surge of affection for this boy who was little more than a stranger. He was risking his life for us. Ivan-I-Am-Not, too. How incredibly brave they were.

Grandmother elbowed me and pointed. Rising above a drab-looking box of a building was most certainly our destination. A huge castle-like structure loomed, taking up nearly an entire block. At the corners of the building were turrets, round with blackened areas that had to be windows. No light came from the structure, at least not from the upper floors. "That's it," Grandmother whispered, though we'd all pretty much figured that out. No wonder she could remember it so clearly!

"Beautiful," Ivan-I-Am-Not said, gawking up at the building. I started to ask Grandmother how the elf could afford such extravagance. Surely a building like that, smack dab in the middle of Manhattan, would cost millions. Then the answer occurred to me. If you had the ability to travel through time, imagine the advantages that would give you. The elf could get the lottery number and travel back and play it. He could pick out the best stocks and travel back and buy them when they were cheap. He could bet on Super Bowls and horse races and World Series games. He could seek out people like Thomas Edison, Alexander Graham Bell, Steve Jobs, and Bill Gates and invest in their inventions. Becoming fabulously wealthy would take no time at all.

"Come on," Ray hissed. He was several yards ahead as we stared dumbly at the castle.

My blood ran cold when a voice in the distance shouted, "Halt!" I should have run, but I instinctively turned to look. A man, dressed in black so that he blended into the night, hurried up the street. He carried something that looked like a weapon. As he drew closer, I recognized it as being similar to the machine Ray and Ivan-I-Am-Not had used on me. He aimed the weapon our way and I felt that strange paralyzing sensation. My head felt fuzzy, my skin clammy. I fought with all my might, but my arms and legs seemed to weigh a hundred pounds each. Grandmother dragged me toward the castle. Though farther from the machine, Ray and Ivan-I-Am-Not staggered like they'd been drugged. "I said halt!" the man shouted.

The machine made me feel like I was running through neck-high water. I needed to fight it, to use my powers. Though I knew doing so would alert the authorities that a Defender had penetrated their defenses. I fought with everything I had to form a North Pulse. This little man, with his little weapon, was not going to stop me. I circled my hand and held out my cane to direct the blast. Ray and

Ivan-I-Am-Not stood paralyzed. The man approached swiftly. Grandmother stepped forward, unaffected by the machine. I wondered vaguely if she was going to try and fight him off herself. I couldn't allow that. She would get hurt. The man was fifty feet away now. My North Pulse was ready. There was no other choice.

No, Carol, Grandmother said. *They'll come for us.*

But I drew back my cane. The man hesitated. So did I. We stared at each other, neither sure what to do. The man looked around, as if hoping for backup. He edged forward and light from a streetlamp illuminated his face. I recognized him! Toby Wise, one of the Defenders I'd fought alongside protecting Santa. He was from Australia and a nice enough guy. He'd spoken only a few words to me, though they'd been nothing but kind. So in this world he was working with the enemy? How depressing that good people could be so easily corrupted.

I was about to fire my North Pulse, regardless of the consequences, when from out of nowhere, a man wearing a mask slammed into Toby, tackling him around the waist. The two of them toppled to the sidewalk. Toby grunted in pain. The weapon went flying and broke into pieces. Ray,

Ivan-I-Am-Not, and I were now free of its effects, but we stood frozen, watching the two men grapple. Our rescuer got the upper hand, using his legs to pin Toby across the chest. He reared back and walloped him. Toby lay still. The mystery man stood and turned to us. He took a step forward. We took a step back. The man pulled off his mask.

I gasped. "Mr. Winters."

He waved us toward him. "Help me," he hissed. Mr. Winters grabbed Toby's arms and pulled him toward the alley from which he'd sprung. We rushed over. Grandmother picked up the remains of the weapon. Ray checked for more cameras. Ivan-I-Am-Not and I helped Mr. Winters drag the unconscious man.

"You came," I said. I wanted to hug him.

"To protect my boys," he said gruffly. "I don't care what you people do."

I smiled. My uncle's world had hardened this version of Mr. Winters, but I suspected he *did* care what happened to us. "Well, thank you anyway."

Mr. Winters grunted and pulled out a rope, tying Toby's hands behind his back. He took a piece of cloth from his pocket and gagged him. "You found the place you're looking for?" Mr. Winters asked.

"A block away," Grandmother said. "The big house."

Mr. Winters nodded. "Let's go then."

Down the street we crept, sticking to the shadows, avoiding the ever-present cameras. Mr. Winters led the way now. We saw no more men in black and we reached the castle within a couple of minutes. We hid across the street from the massive structure, which was even more awe-inspiring up close. An imposing iron fence ringed the elf's home. A huge metal chain with an equally huge padlock hung from the front gate. "Now what?" I whispered.

"Leave it to me," Ivan-I-Am-Not answered, and before any of us could object, he dashed across the street.

Mr. Winters started to chase after him, but Ray grabbed his arm. "Let him do it." Mr. Winters sighed and sank back down, and we watched Ivan-I-Am-Not pull a thin object from his pocket and go to work on the lock. The elf's castle was so large that the front gate was left in dark shadows, which concealed Ivan-I-Am-Not. Within seconds, the lock clicked open. Ivan-I-Am-Not pulled the chain slowly out of the iron gate, lifting it carefully so metal didn't clang against metal. He gently placed it on the sidewalk and waved us over.

"How did you do that?" I whispered as we reached our grinning lockpicker.

"When a person lives in the street, he learns many things." I gave him a hug. If we were able to change things back, I hoped I would find these two boys in my world. As briefly as we'd known each other, I'd already come to think of them as friends.

Mr. Winters grabbed the iron gate and swung it open. It creaked softly, but no one came. The street was deserted. Ray was looking this way and that, up and down, searching for cameras. Mr. Winters, hands on his hips, stared at the castle. Grandmother breathed heavily beside me. Without giving it a second thought (a bad habit of mine), I stepped through the open gate.

"Wait, m'lady!" Mr. Winters whispered.

But it was too late. The moment my foot stepped onto the elf's property, the building exploded in light. Sirens wailed. Windows up and down the block lit up. An engine roared to life in the distance. A crash came from inside the castle. Mr. Winters looked around in panic. He turned to

Grandmother and me. "You two, hide on the grounds. The three of us will draw them away."

"No!" I shouted over the din. "They'll capture you. Come with us."

Mr. Winters stared hard at me. There was a glimmer of something in his eye, a spark that hadn't been there before. "You're sure you can save us?" He spoke so softly I could barely hear him over the alarms. He looked more like the Mr. Winters I knew than he ever had.

I took a deep breath. Shouts could be heard in the distance. A door slammed inside the castle. "I'm sure."

He bowed grandly, as he had so many times before, a knight before the queen. "Then we will trust you to do so, m'lady."

He and the two boys started to take off. But Grandmother grabbed Ray's arm. He looked surprised. "We need him," she said sternly.

"What? Why?" Mr. Winters asked. He looked up and down the street. More engines roared to life.

"I can't explain now," Grandmother said. "Please, just trust me. Carol will keep him safe."

Mr. Winters hesitated. He looked at Ray with a mix of desperation and uncertainty. My heart panged for him. He clearly loved these boys. "OK," he finally said. Ray looked stunned and Mr. Winters pulled him into a quick, violent hug. Ivan-I-Am-Not hugged Ray, too. He hugged me next, flashing an ornery grin. "I wish you the best of luck." Then they were off, sprinting down the street, toward the sound of the shouting.

"Quickly, children," Grandmother said. "We must hide." We ran onto the grounds. I turned to give Mr. Winters and Ivan-I-Am-Not one final look. As I watched them vanish, I wondered if I'd ever see them again. In this world or any other.

CHAPTER 6

The Shimmering Elf

That's him? I asked Grandmother. We hid in thick shrubbery near the corner of the castle, about twenty-five feet from the front door. A small man stood at the front gate talking to one of the security personnel who came running after I'd triggered the alarm. We caught snippets of their conversation.

"A man and a boy. We got them three blocks from here." I felt sick to my stomach.

"What were they doing?"

"We don't know . . ." They moved farther into the street and the conversation was lost to the night.

Does that look like an elf, dear? I tried hard not to be hurt by her tone, which came through even telepathically.

I can't see him very well.

You'll know the moment you see him.

Why?

No time to explain. She spoke aloud to include Ray. "We need to get inside."

I studied the house. "How?"

"I don't know," Grandmother said. "Maybe climb a gutter and enter through the roof somehow?"

We looked for handholds, but I didn't think that was such a hot idea. How would the Ancient One climb up the side of a building at her age? "We don't know if there's even an entrance up there," I responded. "You're sure you can't use a portal?"

"He would vanish at the sight of me. Let's just say we weren't friends."

I wondered again why on Earth he would help us if he hated Grandmother so much. But I kept that to myself. I had to pick my battles with her. "We could create another distraction and run through the front door," I suggested.

"Maybe," Grandmother said. "Or perhaps there's a basement or cellar we could get in through."

"Or maybe I could freeze time for a few seconds. They might think it's Mr. Winters if they detect it."

"Too risky," Grandmother answered. "Maybe . . ."

"Maybe . . ." Ray interrupted. He'd been so silent, crouching behind us, that the sound of his voice made me jump. "*Maybe*," he repeated, "we could go through this open window." He stood next to a large window that swung inward. He pushed it in farther to emphasize his point. His grin was clear, even in the shadows.

"Yeah, I guess we could do that," I said, grinning back.

Ray pulled himself into the window and tumbled to the floor inside. He scrambled to his feet and his face appeared above the windowsill. He reached for Grandmother. "You're next, ma'am."

Grandmother smiled. "Such a gentleman." Ray pulled her up and I lifted from behind. Then the two of them helped me. We stood in a dark room. My eyes had yet to adjust. The air seemed stale, like a musty basement. Ray closed the window and pulled the curtains shut. Now it was pitch-black, but he flipped on a small flashlight he pulled from his pocket.

Grandmother gasped, and I followed the track of her eyes through the gloom. Ray directed the light in the same direction. Two mannequin-like figures, wearing crowns and the long robes of elven royalty, stared back at us. The mannequins looked so real I suspected they weren't mannequins at all but wax figures like the ones at Madame Tussaud's famous museum. Their regal faces took me back to my first encounters with the king and queen and how much their beauty and power had intimidated me. "That weasel," Grandmother muttered.

"What?" I asked.

"He must have betrayed them." Grandmother stroked the plush material of the royal robes. "How else would he get these?" She took the light from Ray and scanned the room, revealing more artifacts. There were old wooden trains, baby dolls, blocks and all kinds of playthings. On the wall hung a reindeer harness, which made my blood boil. What had happened to Santa's poor reindeer and what did the elf have to do with it?

But that was nothing. In a glass case in the center of the room sat something that made me want to scream. Santa's hat, bright red and snow white, glowed in the beam of Ray's flashlight. "He took Santa's cap?" I asked, hardly able to process how horrible that was. What kind of monster were we asking for help? Ray had moved close to the case. "It's real," he muttered. "I can't believe it's actually real."

"Why would he even want these things?" I asked, wishing we could be anywhere but this room.

"He was bitter and angry when we expelled him from the kingdom," Grandmother answered. "A perfect candidate for your uncle to manipulate." Grandmother handed the light back to Ray. "Come on, let's find him," she huffed. Her face was bright red, so much so that she looked possessed, like an elven demon. "You go first. If I see him, I'm not sure what I'll do." I'd never seen Grandmother so angry. It scared me.

Ray took one last yearning look at Santa's hat. We snuck out of the artifact room and crept down a long hall-way. Paintings and pieces of weird-looking art lined the walls. In our studies, Grandmother had forced me to read art history books and I recognized the style of a painting of a woman. She had geometric shapes for a face and eyes that were off-center yet somehow made perfect sense. *Is that a Picasso?* I asked.

I believe so.

I guess not everything's changed if he's a famous artist here, too, I said, comforted by the thought.

It's hard to know what stayed the same and what was altered. The ripples of time are unpredictable. That's why it's incredibly dangerous to travel back. When I get my hands on that little skunk . . .

But couldn't we mess things up even worse going back?

Maybe. But we don't have a choice after what your uncle did.

I felt bad talking to Grandmother and not including Ray in the conversation, but we needed to stay as quiet as possible. And he didn't seem to say a whole lot anyway, unlike his chatty friend. Thinking of Ivan-I-Am-Not made me cringe. Where were they? And what sort of punishment awaited them? I hoped my uncle didn't hurt them, but that was probably a futile wish.

At the end of the long hall, we came to a set of huge double doors. We paused to study them and peer behind us to make sure we weren't being followed. "Open it?" Ray whispered, and Grandmother nodded. She hung back in case the elf waited on the other side. Ray pulled the door open slowly, the creaking hinges making us wince. A blast of frigid air enveloped us, and what the opening door revealed made our jaws drop.

Grandmother forgot herself and stepped forward. I was too mesmerized to think of pushing her back. Before us was a grand ballroom, with high ceilings and an enormous chandelier hanging in the center. But where a dance floor or banquet tables should have been was instead a winter wonderland. There were benches, slides, igloo-like houses and sculptures, all made of ice. Not the beautiful blue ice of the North Pole, but close enough to make me homesick for the lost kingdom. A large tree stood in the center, around which the ice flowed this way and that. The room was the elf kingdom in miniature. A tear trickled down Grandmother's cheek and she wiped it away. Ray stared silently. I wished he could see the real elf kingdom in all its glory, not this pale imitation.

Then I noticed a hunched-over figure on the other side of the icescape, sitting on a bench and looking up at a sculpture of a female elf with a child at her side. The woman was young and beautiful, the boy resembling her, and the bent figure kept his focus locked on the sculpture, as if he expected the woman and child to spring to life. My eyes must have been playing tricks on me because the seated figure suddenly shimmered. He rose up straight and tall on the bench. Then he shimmered again and sat back down. Grandmother pulled us out of sight of the figure. The artificial snow crunched under my feet. Our breath puffed like steam engines.

"That's him?" I whispered.

Grandmother nodded. I peeked around and the elf shimmered again, almost as if he were fading away and then back again. It definitely wasn't my eyes playing tricks. "What's wrong with him?" I asked.

"Never mind that now," Grandmother said. "You need to talk to him."

"What do I say?" My stomach had twisted into a giant pretzel. If the shimmering, traitorous "weasel" of an elf was the only one who could help us go back and fix everything, the world as I once knew it depended on this moment. Depended on me.

"Tell him who you are as calmly as you can," Grandmother said. "Don't accuse him of anything. Just state your case. Build his trust. Ray will go with you." She turned to him. "Let Carol do the talking, OK?" Ray nodded. She turned back to me. "Are you ready?"

"I guess." The three of us snuck close. It wasn't difficult because of all the ice structures to hide behind. Only the soft crunch of the snow under our feet made any sound. The elf seemed lost in his own world. As we drew closer, step by icy step, I realized he was talking aloud, looking up at the mother and child sculpture, as if he were having a conversation with them. I thought of my friend Ramon, the Defender we'd lost on our rescue mission to the Dominican Republic. When we returned from our trip, all of us devastated by the loss, Santa had a memorial stone erected out past the reindeer barn. Sometimes I'd talk to Ramon, or to his stone anyway. I hoped he was somewhere listening. It made me feel better to believe he was. This struck me as the same sort of thing, the elf talking to loved ones no longer around. His wife and son?

About twenty feet away, Grandmother stopped us behind a large ice house. She gave me a nudge and I approached the shimmering elf from behind, Ray at my heels. I was about five feet from him when the elf finally realized he had an intruder. He jumped off the bench and spun to face me. He started to make a portal, but I yelled, "Wait!" He shimmered, and it seemed to stagger him like a punch. When I saw up close what was happening, the blood rushed to my head and I thought I might faint. Ray took in a sharp breath and stepped back.

The elf's face changed. Actually, his whole body changed. He was a bent old wrinkled elf, much like Grandmother, when he suddenly shifted into a young, handsome elf, strong and tall, with flowing silver hair. Then he shifted again, this time into middle age, his face morphing with his body. "Who are you?" he yelled, his hands poised to create a portal. I started to answer and he shifted once more, this time so dramatically I stepped back next to Ray. Our shoulders touched and I felt him trembling. The elf was now a child, sweet-faced and innocent, despite the fierce scowl he directed at us. "I said who are you?" he repeated in the high-pitched voice of a young elf.

"My name is Carol," I answered. A thought occurred to me, maybe a way for him to trust me. *They call me Christmas Carol,* I said telepathically. The elf looked startled. *I come from the world that used to exist.*

He shimmered back into an elderly version, though not quite as old this time. *What do you want from me? I didn't do it. He did.*

I knew who *he* was, but there was no use pointing out that my uncle never could have done what he did without the elf's help, or that the elf shouldn't have been messing with time in the first place. *I know he did*, I answered, trying to sound sympathetic. *The Supreme Leader is my uncle.*

The elf's eyes widened. He shimmered into a middle-age version. I wondered how many versions of him there were. *You're . . . Carol.*

That's what I said.

He told me you were ungrateful, that you turned on him and tried to destroy everything he created.

"He lies!" I shouted, striding forward. "He betrayed me! He betrayed everyone!"

The elf shrank from my fury and I forced myself to take a breath. My face burned so hot, I imagined I could melt his entire winter world with just a look. "He said he would help me," the elf whimpered. "He said he could bring them back." He glanced at the ice sculpture. The female elf was beautiful, with long flowing hair that sparkled as ice. The child looked a lot like the young version of the elf.

"He lies," I said again. The elf hung his head and cried. Even though I knew the awful things he'd done, even though I'd seen the evidence of his betrayal, I felt sorry for him. He was pathetic. I put my arms around him. He flinched and tried to pull away. But I held tight.

"What happened to them?" I asked. He shimmered and shifted as my arms embraced him. Such a strange sensation.

The elf was young and vibrant again, probably about the same age as the female in the sculpture. He wiped his cheeks. He looked disgusted with himself.

"He lost them," came my grandmother's voice. She stepped from her hiding place. "He played around with forces he should have left alone and he lost them."

"You!" The elf's face transformed again, not into a younger or older version, but into rage. He backed away, but I grabbed his hand. He turned old again, and feeble, and I gripped him hard.

"Please, wait," I said. "We need your help."

"I'm done helping anyone," he snapped. "No one's ever helped me get them back." He was young again, and strong, and he yanked away from me. A portal appeared before him.

"I'll find them," I shouted in desperation. "I know I can. And you'll be a family again." The elf's portal crackled, and he looked at me with a glimmer of something in his eyes. Hope?

"I don't know, Carol," Grandmother said. "It's dangerous. Bad enough you have to go back in time at all."

The elf leaned toward his portal, ready to bolt. "How will you find them? You're just a child."

I crossed my arms and glared. "I'm sick of people saying that. I'm a Defender of Claus who saved Santa. And I have elf blood, too. If anyone can do it, I can."

"And why should I trust you?" he asked. "You're with the elf who had me expelled from the kingdom."

"You brought that on yourself," Grandmother snapped. "You know that."

"I just wanted to find them."

"And look what that's gotten you. Look at the terrible world you created."

The elf said nothing. He looked longingly at the portal, the reflection of it making his eyes seem like they were on fire. There was anguish in every feature of his shimmering face. "I'll do it!" he finally said. "Let's do it right now."

"No way!" I responded. "Only after you've helped us." The elf certainly hadn't shown he could be trusted.

And who knew how long it would take to find his family, or if I even could. But I would try if he helped us change things back. I would keep my promise. The elf hung his head again. The portal vanished. He slumped back on the bench and looked up at the ice sculpture. "Please find them," he whispered. "Please."

The way he traveled back in time surprised me. I expected some sort of elaborate elven magic. I guess it technically was. But to achieve the magic, the elf had built a machine that looked like a huge ray gun.

"You know how you make a portal by forming a circle with your hands and concentrating on your destination?" he asked. The elf's mood had changed for the better. He seemed excited to demonstrate how the machine worked, like a mad scientist showing off a discovery, blind to the fact it might destroy the planet.

"Yes," Grandmother and I answered in unison. Ray said nothing. He seemed overwhelmed. I sure couldn't blame him for that.

"Well, I figured out that if you make a spiral instead, smaller and smaller, over and over again, you can drill a hole through time."

"How do you control where you go?" I asked.

"Ah, now that's the trick," the elf said. He shimmered into the kid version of himself. As weird as it was seeing him change, I was getting used to it. "It's not an exact science. The first time I managed to travel back, I thought I'd failed. Nothing changed. Then I saw an earlier version of myself coming home from the toy factory after a day of work. I'd gone back an hour." The elf powered up the machine, which shimmied and coughed, as if it hadn't been used in a long time. After a loud crack that sounded like a car backfiring, the contraption hummed like an electric powerline, throbbing slightly, as if it had a heartbeat.

"What happened to your family?" I had been trying to work up the courage and wondered if I should even ask. But if I was going to try and find them, I needed to know.

The elf dropped his head. He was elderly now, beaten down by his long life. "We lost the child," he said softly. "A terrible accident. I wanted to go back and prevent it.

And after countless tries, it worked. My wife and I went and got him. Can you imagine the joy of being reunited with someone you lost?" I thought of my mother, who had died when I was five. How wonderful it would be to have her embrace me once again. That kind of temptation would be difficult to resist. "But when I tried to send them back to the present, they vanished. I don't know what happened. I've been looking for them since."

He shimmered into his youthful, strong self. Ray spoke up behind me, the sound of his voice making me jump again. "Why does that keep happening to you?"

The elf didn't answer. He glanced at Grandmother, who glared at him. The elf slumped his shoulders. He looked like a little kid who'd finally admitted to his mom that he'd broken her favorite vase. "It's why I was exiled. I refused to stop searching for them. And to go back so many times, there are . . ." He seemed to be trying to come up with the right word. "Consequences. For elves in particular."

"What do you mean?" I asked.

"Every time he goes back, he merges with the version of himself that exists in that time period," Grandmother said. "Two versions of the same elf can't exist at the same time."

It made sense now, how he kept shimmering into so many variations of himself. "How many times have you gone back?"

The elf hesitated, glancing at Grandmother once more, as if he'd broken a whole shelf full of vases.

"How many?" she asked sternly.

"Ninety-eight."

"Good heavens!" Grandmother said. "You're lucky to be alive."

"If I can't find my family, I don't care about living," the elf said.

"You have other children," Grandmother said.

"They don't speak to me after I was exiled." He scowled at Grandmother. "Thanks to you."

"Don't you dare put that on me, you miserable old elf!" Grandmother stormed over to him. "I'm not the one who messed around with time and caused such a disaster." The red-faced elves stood nose to nose. I honestly thought she might slap him.

"It's not fair!" he shouted. "I couldn't bear losing them."

"OK, OK," I said, stepping between them. "He made

a mistake. You can understand why he did it. Right, Grandmother?"

She breathed like an angry bull but took a step back. "Everyone loses people. He's no different from the rest of us. It's the way of things, and no one should fool around with that."

"But what about when I reversed time to save Santa and the Defenders?" I asked. Grandmother said nothing to that. "He understands what he's done," I said softly. "He's learned his lesson. Haven't you?" The elf nodded, a bit unconvincingly. "We need you to send us back to the same time you sent my uncle. We need to undo what he did."

The elf was still angry. "Why should I care what happened to the rest of the world? The world never cared about me."

"Baloney," Grandmother said.

I put my hand on her shoulder. I did the same to the shimmering elf. "Do you know what happened to the elf kingdom?" I asked him.

"I don't care," he snapped.

"My uncle destroyed it. It's wrecked."

The elf shrugged. "Your girls were there," Grandmother said. "Who knows what happened to them or where they are."

The elf squirmed and pulled away from me. "They were dead to me a long time ago."

I held out my cane and began to make a portal, concentrating on making one so big he could see the entire elf kingdom, or what was left of it. He cringed when the crumbling ice and splintered tree appeared. "This is what I want to fix. And then I'll help you. I can make a portal stronger than any other elf and my cane focuses that power. If anyone can find your wife and son, I can."

"How do I know you won't trick me? The more I think about it, the more I think you're just using me for what you want and I'll never see you again."

"Not everyone's a traitorous weasel like you," Grandmother snapped, and she was in his face once more.

Grandmother! I said telepathically. *You're not helping.* I gently pulled her back and kept my hand on her shoulder. "I promise I'll help you," I said. "I will find them."

"Send them back," Grandmother said. "You can trust her."

The elf clenched his jaw so tight I thought his face might crack. He glared at Grandmother but finally said, "OK."

At first I was relieved. Then something Grandmother said registered in my brain. "Wait, what do you mean send *them* back? You mean us. The three of us."

Grandmother looked away. "I can't go, dear. Merging with my younger self like that, I think it would kill me."

"But I need you," I said. "I can't do this alone."

She pointed to Ray. "That's why I asked him to come. And you two will be fine since you didn't exist during the time period your uncle went back to." She glanced questioningly at the elf.

"They would be OK," he said.

"So it's settled then," Grandmother said. "You will help Ray and Carol go back, and Carol will help find your family when she's undone all this damage."

The shimmering elf hadn't actually agreed to the plan—and neither had I, for that matter—but Grandmother had a knack for getting her way. She glared hard at the elf, who shimmered into the elderly version, and at last, he nodded. Ray and I were headed back in time.

CHAPTER 7

1851

It's pretty weird when someone sitting right in front of you says, "Go find me." But that's what Grandmother told me I needed to do once Ray and I traveled through time and arrived at our destination. "She'll help you."

"But you, um, she won't even know me," I argued. Again, sooooo weird, my Earlier Grandmother not even knowing who I am. And my Now Grandmother telling me to go find my Earlier Grandmother to seek help. I really thought my head might explode. "What do I say to her?"

"Hmm. That's a good point." She thought about it, lightly tapping her foot in the artificial snow. Ray sat in silence, clenching and unclenching his fists as he watched the elf fiddle with the machine. He probably hadn't bar-

119

gained on time travel when he agreed to help. "Tell her that Santa forgives her," Grandmother said.

I wrinkled my brow. "What does that mean?"

"It has to do with something I've . . . we've, never told anyone."

"What?"

Grandmother smiled, but it was a sad smile, one of regret. "We all have our secrets, dearest. You don't need to know all of mine." I suppose it didn't matter as long as Earlier Grandmother knew what I was talking about, but I was beyond curious.

We were traveling to December 20, 1851, two days before my uncle had been sent back by the shimmering elf. When the elf told us the date Uncle Christopher requested, Grandmother's eyes grew wide with recognition.

"You remember that time?" I asked.

"Like it was yesterday."

"How do you remember some random day almost 270 years ago?" I asked.

Grandmother rolled her eyes. "We need to add more math to your schooling, dear. It's *170* years."

"Oh, right. But how do you remember that?" I didn't

say what I was thinking: *When you couldn't even remember what block the mean elf lived on.* Thank goodness I'd learned to protect my thoughts from other elves.

"You don't forget the time you recruited the very first Defender," Grandmother said. "Santa's coming to find me on December 22, and you need to be in Seneca Village when he arrives. Just remember that name."

Ray sat forward, his eyes aglow. "We get to meet Santa?" The absolute joy on his face made me smile. He looked like a little kid on Christmas Eve, imagining Santa and his reindeer landing on the roof.

"Yes, Ray, you get to meet Santa," Grandmother said, smiling along with me.

"But if Santa was mad at you, why did he come?" I asked.

Grandmother looked pained. "He needed an elf who knew the lives of humans," she said. "I was his only option." The shimmering elf glanced at her and snorted.

"For what?" I asked.

The elf stopped working on his machine. "She became the Defender hunter," he said, shifting from a child to an elderly version.

"*Hunter's* the wrong word," Grandmother said, frowning. "I'd say *recruiter*. And I had to make up for . . ." she cut herself short. "Santa or I would sense them, and I would track them down and bring them back. Only if they were willing, of course. Sort of like Mr. Winters did for you, Carol. Santa needed them for his plan, his vision of what he'd become."

My mind raced. Grandmother had helped create the Defenders of Claus! "Why didn't you ever tell me that?" I asked, exasperated.

"Didn't seem important."

"Not important?! You're responsible for the Defenders of Claus!" Then my thoughts leaped to something else, something terrible. "Wait, if Santa still exists in this world but the Defenders don't, and you were the one who found them, that means . . ." I hesitated, hardly able to bear the idea.

"What?" Ray asked. Grandmother looked away.

"The Supreme Leader targeted her," the shimmering elf said. "And by the way things turned out, I'd say he must have gotten her." He laughed, and it was all I could do to keep from firing a North Pulse right at his stupid shimmering head.

"You're a jerk," I said.

"She got me kicked out of the kingdom," he hissed. "What do I care? And how was I supposed to know what your crazy uncle was going to do? You think he shared his plans with me?"

Grandmother held up her hand for silence. "None of it matters, because Carol's going to stop him. And protecting the first Defender is the key. He'll need convincing."

"What do you mean?" I asked.

She hesitated. "Telling you too much is dangerous, Carol. If you reveal details about the future to those in the past, there could be horrible consequences. You can't tell them who you are or that you're my granddaughter."

"OK, OK, but what do you mean about the first Defender?"

Grandmother sighed. "Just know that he could have taken a different path, and I wouldn't have blamed him if he had."

"I don't understand," I said.

"Follow Santa's lead. You'll find out soon enough. If Santa succeeds like he's supposed to and you stop your uncle, the Defenders will be formed and all this unpleasantness will go away." The elf snorted and went back to work on his machine. Ray clenched and unclenched his fists. And my mind churned. This wasn't going to be easy.

"How are we going to get home?" I asked Grandmother. The elf had nearly finished preparing his machine, and all the nerves in my body seemed to have found their way to my stomach and twisted themselves into a tight knot. My skin felt clammy, even in the elf's artificial frozen world.

"I'll make him come for you," she said. "And he will if he wants his family back. When I see that history's altered, I'll send him."

"I don't trust him," I whispered. "What if he changes his mind and we're stuck?"

"That's the chance we'll have to take, Carol."

Grandmother wasn't one to sugarcoat anything. She knew what Ray and I were getting into, and that it might end badly. I knew, too. From the very beginning, Mr. Winters had warned me of the dangers of becoming a Defender, though probably even he couldn't have imagined this kind of catastrophe.

"Ready," the shimmering elf called. Ray stood and his knees buckled. He looked about as nervous as I felt. I wanted to give him a reassuring hug, but I wouldn't have known what to say. The elf flipped switches on the machine's control panel. The knot in my stomach tightened.

"Hold on," Grandmother said. "I need to make a portal."

"Why?" I asked.

"When things change again, I want to be outside the time continuum."

"Oh, yeah." It was just like when my uncle went back and Grandmother pulled us into a portal to keep us safe from the changes he was making. My head swam. The rules of this game were so confusing.

Grandmother hugged Ray, patting him lightly on the back. Next, she pulled me close. "Good luck, my dearest," she whispered. "I have faith in you."

"I'm glad *you* do," I said, trying to make a joke.

Her smile disappeared, and she fixed her gaze on me. "I have faith in you," she repeated, sternly this time.

I stood straighter and let my smile slip away. "I'll try my best."

"That's all any of us can do, sweetheart." She hugged me even tighter.

The shimmering elf pointed to a metal archway. "When I tell you, run into the time portal."

"Explain it to me," I said, gripping my cane. Its pulsing power reassured me.

The elf sighed, as if he couldn't be bothered. But I glared at him. "It's similar to making a portal, except instead of bringing your hands together to form a circle, you take one hand and make a spiral. Just like with a portal, you focus on something specific where you want to go. Or in this case, *when* you want to go. You make the spiral over and over, until it cuts through time."

"So you're like a drill," Ray said.

"Yes," the elf responded. "It takes practice, and the older I get the more difficult it becomes. But the machine I built focuses my energy, making it more precise. It's as if it gets to the core of my power and amplifies it. Once it does, I'm able to drill through time."

"OK," I nodded. "Thank you."

The elf grunted and shifted into a child, which kind of freaked me out. Nothing like putting your lives into the hands of a little kid. But I knew the old elf was in there.

The elf flipped one last switch on the machine and it roared to life, getting louder and louder. He stepped in front of it and waited. A beam shot from the machine and the elf stiffened, as if his body was being filled with energy. The elf then stepped toward the archway. He squeezed his eyes shut. He began making the spiral with his hand, as if he'd done it a thousand times.

Grandmother stood next to the normal portal she'd made and watched. Her eyes welled up and I had to look away to keep from crying myself. If I failed, we'd never see each other again. The elf's hand went faster and faster. He shimmered into version after version of himself. He drilled through time, further and further. "Almost," the elf said through clenched teeth. A massive portal materialized in the archway. But with this portal, I couldn't see what was on the other side. All I could see was a spinning vortex, like water going down a drain. How brave, or foolish, or desperate the elf must have been to leap into the unknown the first time he tried this. "Now!" the elf yelled.

I glanced at Grandmother once more. She waved and jumped into her portal. I took Ray's hand and pulled him along. Together we bolted through the archway, into history.

For just a moment, I thought the elf had failed. There he stood, shimmering from old to young, right in front of us, in the same house we'd just left. But the artificial winter kingdom was gone, in its place a normal ballroom with dozens of round tables, each surrounded by chairs. And light streamed through the ballroom windows; it was daytime, not night. The third clue was how the elf was dressed. Instead of his drab, standard-issue gray uniform, he wore a brown tweed suit.

The elf had made a portal and looked poised to flee. "Who are you?" he snapped. "Why are you in my house?"

Ray promptly barfed on the ballroom floor. I felt wobbly myself. But in my life as a Defender, I had grown accustomed to portal trips, and Pole vaults, and rides on the backs of huge reindeer. I patted Ray's back as he bent over and puked again. The elf looked at him with disgust.

"You sent us," I said hurriedly as the elf leaned toward his escape portal. I chose not to mention the fact that we had forced him to.

"And why would I do that?" the elf asked. His lip curled into a snarl. It didn't seem possible, but he was even nastier in the past. He shimmered into his older self.

"I promised to help find your family."

His eyes rounded. The snarl vanished. He let the portal disintegrate. "And how can some freckle-faced brat do what I haven't been able to?"

"That's none of your concern right now," I snapped. What a nasty piece of work he was! "I'm not doing *anything* until you help us undo what you've done."

"What are you talking about? I want you out of my house."

I started to argue, just to be obstinate, to give him as hard a time as he was giving us. Grandmother liked to say, "Carol, you're the most pigheaded elf AND human I've ever seen." But in truth, we didn't really need this elf's help, at least not now. Except for a single piece of vital information. "We'll leave if you tell us one thing."

I'll tell you something all right, he said in his mind, not bothering to hide his thoughts around a couple of humans. *I'll make a portal and drop you in the middle of New York Harbor.*

I smiled, and with every ounce of telepathic power I could muster, I yelled, *NO YOU WON'T, YOU BIG JERK!!*

The elf let out a high-pitched shriek and stumbled backward, falling over a table and chairs. I stepped toward him and waved my hands through the air, freezing him where he lay. All except his head. That was a trick I'd picked up from my father during our practices. "Excellent for asking questions," Dad had explained.

"You mean for interrogating someone," I had responded, making him laugh.

The elf struggled, cursing telepathically and out loud. Ray watched with awe. "How are you doing that?"

"I told you I had power," I said simply, turning back to the elf. "Now, all we want to know is where to find an old friend of yours."

"Who?"

I almost said, "My grandmother," but caught myself. "Noelle."

The elf's face scrunched in disgust. "She's no friend."

"Whatever," I snapped. "She lives near here. Where?" The elf glared. "Where?!" I screamed and froze everything but his lips.

"OK, OK," the elf shouted as best he could with jaws that didn't work. "Four blocks away, living with that mixed-breed granddaughter of hers."

My heart fluttered. Granddaughter? That would be another of my grandmothers. It would be sooooo cool to meet her, even if I couldn't tell her who I was.

"Carol!" Ray shouted. I'd relaxed my grip on the elf. He was back on his feet and had made a portal. I froze him again. "Tell us where," I said. "Or I'll leave you like this for a few days." I didn't actually have that ability, not unless I sat in the room with him the whole time. But he didn't know that. "As a matter of fact, you can take us there. I don't trust you." I relaxed my hold on the elf but held my cane out as a warning. "If you try anything, I'll make a portal and drop *you* in the middle of New York Harbor." Ray stared at me with eyes wide. ˙

The elf's shoulders slumped. He cursed once more for good measure. "Follow me," he grumbled, and out we went into 1851 New York City.

CHAPTER 8

The First Defender

The first thing I noticed was the smell. Yuck! Like sewage, or rotting meat, or wet garbage. The streets were cobblestone and dotted with muddy-looking puddles. Horses pulling rumbling carriages clip-clopped on the stones. And where there were horses, there were piles of what horses left behind. A man carrying a large pot and a shovel strolled down the street, scooping up the droppings and dumping them into his pot. That was an actual job in 1851? Disgusting!

As for the non-poop-scooping people on the street, they all stared at us. It was easy to see why. To them, we were dressed like freaks. The women of 1851 wore over-sized hats and long dresses with cinched waists, and the men wore suits and roundish-looking hats. But Ray and I had on the gray uniforms of my uncle's world. "That girl's wearing bloomers," one woman said. I had no idea what she was talking about. "Scandalous," another said. I avoided eye contact, hoping they would leave us to our business.

Walking down the street, it certainly didn't feel like New York City. There wasn't a single skyscraper. Most buildings were wooden and no higher than three or four stories. Houses were built close together, but a few larger ones actually had yards. One structure took up about a fourth of a block and seemed to be a general store. In the windows were boxes of something called Old Man Murray's All Natural Soap. And next to those were John Godwin's Miracle Tonic, bottles and bottles of it. "Cures all ails," the bottle proclaimed, which was a bit hard to believe. Glancing inside the store, I could see baskets full of potatoes, radishes, carrots, and dried beans, along with packages of flour and sugar stacked at least twenty high. I really wanted to go in and check it out, but the elf was hurrying down the street. I had to force myself to look away and not lose track of him.

On the wall of the general store was pasted a poster that read, Miss Jenny Lind, Swedish opera sensation. Presented by P.T. Barnum. I knew that name! Barnum was the guy who founded the famous circus. I wished we had time to go see Miss Jenny Lind. I didn't know much about opera, but it would be soooooo cool to see a show in 1851. This was a business trip, however. No time for fun.

We walked for a few blocks, following the nasty elf. He wore a hood to conceal his shimmering, and he glanced back at us repeatedly. I tried to keep my eye on him, figuring he would bolt the first chance he got. But the sights and sounds and smells of the strange new world made that difficult.

Horse-drawn carriages and wagons were everywhere, and some of the wagons carried goods piled high in the back. Sacks of food, I assumed. Maybe flour. One driver steered a fancy carriage with curtains on the windows. He wore a sharp black suit, a top hat, and white gloves and carried himself with an arrogant grace. I wanted to peek inside to see what sort of rich folks could afford such a fancy carriage and such a fancy driver.

On the next corner, dirty-faced boys, with berets on their scruffy heads and their tattered pants held up by suspenders, sold newspapers, shoving them toward prospective customers, some of whom pushed the boys away. "Headless body found in Bowery!" one boy screamed, extending the paper toward us. "Get that away from me," the elf snapped and slapped the paper to the street. The elf's rudeness barely fazed the boy. He stared at me, studying my clothes, then picked up his paper and hurried to his next customer. "Gruesome discovery in the Bowery!" he shouted. "Headless body!"

"Why do you have to be so nasty?" I asked, but the elf ignored me. We stopped in front of a drab four-story wooden building painted brown and covered in a dingy film of dirt and grime. The windows on the first floor were so filthy you couldn't see through them. "Here," the elf said. I turned to ask which apartment Grandmother lived in, only to see him leap into a portal. He was gone in an instant. Someone on the street screamed. Passersby turned to look. "Witch!" a woman shouted and pointed at me. "She's a witch!"

"She made him vanish!" another shouted.

"Devils!" the first woman yelled. Her face screwed up with fury, as if she spotted witches all the time and the sight of them sent her into a rage. She looked like she was about to leap on me. Her teeth were rotten, and when she got in my face, her breath smelled a lot like what the guy was scooping off the street.

The crowd pressed toward us. A policeman with a bushy mustache appeared. He wore a crisp blue uniform, along with a tall blue hat held in place by a chinstrap, and he smacked a billy club threateningly against the palm of his hand. Ray backed away. "I think we'd better get out of here," he muttered.

"I'll take care of it," I said. And with a wave of my hand, I froze time. Everything stopped except for me and Ray.

He stumbled on the step to Grandmother's building, landing hard on his butt. "How do you do that?" He pulled himself up and stared into the face of the angry policeman. He hesitantly touched the officer's bushy mustache and jerked his hand away, as if he expected the officer to grab him.

"Can't you?" I asked.

"All I can do is make Pulses."

"I'll teach you sometime," I said. "Let's go." Up the stairs we went, onto a small porch built in front of a single, windowless door. I tried the knob, expecting the door to be locked, but it swung open. After we disappeared inside, I waved my hand to unfreeze time. "Where'd they go?" someone shouted. "They're witches, I tell you." "Find them, officer!"

The policeman stuttered, "I-I-I- . . . just move along!"

I smiled at Ray in the dim entryway. "You didn't know you were friends with a witch, did you?" He smiled back, and we stumbled down the hall, the flickering lamps on the walls doing little to illuminate our way.

"Almost forgot," Ray said, and he flipped on his flashlight. The fact that there'd be no electricity in 1851 hadn't occurred to me, and I felt stupid for being surprised. When had Thomas Edison invented the light bulb? When did buildings start having electricity and lights that weren't candles or burning oil? Grandmother was right. I needed more schooling.

"Turn that off if you see someone," I said. "They won't have a clue what it is and we can't draw attention to ourselves."

Ray flipped the flashlight off when we approached a door to an apartment. I knocked lightly and heard a shuffling of feet and the clatter of a pan from inside. An elderly woman, who was most definitely not my grandmother, opened the door, eyeing us suspiciously. "What do you want?" she barked.

"We're looking for someone," I said. "Noelle. A small woman living with another woman." I started to mention her granddaughter but remembered that Noelle wouldn't age like a human. Maybe her daughter would stay young-looking, too, but she'd be only part elf. My guess was that Earlier Grandmother didn't look much older than her granddaughter.

"Top floor, first door," the woman snapped and slammed the door in our faces.

"Jeez," I muttered. "Is everyone mean here?"

Ray turned the flashlight back on, and we headed up the stairs. Three flights of creaking, groaning stairs later, we stood outside of Grandmother's apartment. The door was an ordinary brown and needed paint. There was no number and I wondered vaguely how they received their mail. I started to knock but then dropped my hand to my side. I was trembling.

"What's wrong?" Ray asked.

"She won't know me."

He put his hand on my shoulder and squeezed. "Well, you know her and you know she's a good person, or, um, elf. She'll help us. That's all that matters."

"Yeah," I said, even though that wasn't all that mattered to me. Having someone I love not recognize me mattered. The thought of not being able to tell her who I was also mattered. I knocked, trying to still my shaking hand. Ray rocked from side to side, looking nervous despite his reassurances.

When the door opened, I couldn't move. It was as if someone froze *me*. My mouth opened, but no sound came out. Then I started crying. I couldn't help it. The woman who stared back at me was not my mother. She was NOT my mother. But it was as if my mother stood before me, back from the dead, conjured from the few fuzzy memories I had of her. I saw every feature of Mom in this woman's face. Her hair was a golden blonde with hints of silver. Her cheeks were lightly freckled and her skin seemed to glow. She had the perfect little round nose I'd stared at for so many hours in the few pictures I had of Mom. I couldn't stop crying. And this woman, a stranger to me, she did the most amazing thing. "Oh, honey, what's wrong?" she asked and pulled me into a hug, a miraculous embrace. And the tears poured out of me.

I put my arms around her waist and held tight. She smelled like roses and cinnamon. She rubbed my back and caressed my neck. "I'm sorry," I said. I couldn't catch my breath. I snotted all over the front of her pretty dress. But she didn't seem to mind. Just as a mother, *my mother*, wouldn't.

"It's fine, honey. What's troubling you?"

I took a deep breath. I couldn't stop shaking. "You remind me of someone," I said. "A person I lost."

"Oh, honey," she said and hugged me tighter. I closed my eyes and imagined it truly was Mom. My heart swelled. I ached to tell her who I was. "I'm really sorry to hear that." She pulled back and wiped my tears with her thumb. She smiled at Ray and reached over and stroked his cheek, too. I could tell he was trying not to cry. Big tough boy. "Would you two like to come in?" I nodded dumbly. "My name is Elizabeth. What are yours? And to what do I owe this delightful pleasure on such a brisk, wintry day?"

She took us each by the hand and pulled us into the apartment. I stopped in my tracks, sparking a puzzled glance from the sweet woman. She must have thought there was something seriously wrong with me. But if she reminded me of my mother, the apartment reminded me of something I knew even more intimately. It was as if I were standing in Grandmother's house in the North Pole. There was the bed with the antique quilt, the table with three chairs sitting next to the icebox. There was the fireplace with the couch and chair positioned to enjoy the warmth of the crackling flames. There was even a stack of books on the living room table, as if Earlier Grandmother had been expecting me and we'd jump right into my "schooling."

The apartment was decorated beautifully, with fresh green garlands strung over the doorways. A lovely little tree with red balls and silver trinkets sat in the corner. Stockings were hung just as Grandmother had done in her cabin at the North Pole. And then I spotted something that made me burst into tears all over again. On the fireplace mantel, placed in the center to give it more prominence, sat my carved wooden Santa figurine, the one my parents had given me for Christmas right before Mom died. I had no idea the figurine had been passed down through the generations of Mom's family. Maybe she and Dad didn't think I'd care about knowing that. They were wrong. I tried to make myself look away from the figurine, to stop my crying. Elizabeth hugged me again and guided us to a couch. "It's OK, honey," she said as I attempted to compose myself.

Elizabeth sat in a chair across from us, the same chair Dad always occupied at Grandmother's cabin. I wiped my tears away and glanced down. When I looked closely at the books, my heart did another flip-flop. *A Christmas Carol* by Charles Dickens lay on top. I picked it up, cradling it in my hands like a precious object. The book was beautiful, leather-bound, brand-new, not like the tattered copy Mr. Winters and his gang of misfits treasured. I tried not to cry again. I really was embarrassing myself. I took another deep breath. "My name is Carol, and this is Ray, and we're here to see Noelle," I said. "We need her help."

Elizabeth studied us. Her stare lingered on me in particular, and for a second, I caught a hint of what might have been recognition in her eyes. Surely she knew what our grandmother was. Elizabeth was only a quarter elf, and I wondered if she had inherited the telepathy gene. Maybe it skipped generations and I was just lucky to get it. In my head I said, *Can you tell me where she is?*

She jolted like she'd gotten an electric shock and her eyes grew wide. *Who are you?*

"Someone who came a long way to help her," I said aloud.

Elizabeth said nothing. She looked at me with more suspicion than before. "She's seeking someone," she finally said.

"Someone with special abilities," Ray said.

Elizabeth's head jerked toward my friend and her eyes narrowed. "How did you know that?" She was looking more and more suspicious.

"A friend of yours sent us. I can explain everything once we find Noelle. Please," I begged. "Trust us."

She thought about it but must have decided that a couple of kids were no threat. "I don't know where she is at the moment."

"Can you make a portal?" I asked. Because I didn't know this version of Grandmother and she didn't know me, the connection wouldn't be strong enough for me to make one.

"How did you . . . ?" Elizabeth started to ask. "I'm not very good at them."

"If you can show her to me, then I can make a stronger one and go to where she is."

"I'll try," Elizabeth said. She closed her eyes and made a circle in the air with her hands. The portal shimmered in and out of solidity until it appeared long enough for me to get a good look at Grandmother. I smiled. She wasn't exactly young, but she still looked strong and quite beautiful. The portal was weak so Noelle hadn't noticed it, and she walked through what looked like farmland. That confused me. Had she traveled outside the city in her search? Elizabeth's portal collapsed and she slumped over. "I'm sorry. I couldn't hold it."

"That's OK," I said. "I got a good look at her. We can go to her now." Ray groaned and I tried not to laugh. "Don't worry, Ray. This isn't like what we just did. It'll be over in a jiffy." He nodded in resignation, and I made a circle with my hands. "It was very nice to meet you, Elizabeth. I'm sorry I was such a mess."

"Wait," she said. "You can't go dressed like that. Only untoward women wear bloomers."

There was that silly-sounding word again. "What are bloomers?" I asked. And what the heck is *untoward*?

"Trousers," she said, pointing to the pants portion of my uniform. "Wait here." Ray and I glanced at each other. Elizabeth disappeared down the hall and emerged a minute later with a lovely sky blue dress and a simple brown suit and white dress shirt. "This dress is Noelle's. She's about your size." She handed it to me. "And this was my grandfather's," she said to Ray. "Probably a bit big, but better than what you have on." The woman pointed to the back. "There are two rooms in which you can change. And a chamber pot if you need it."

"A what?"

Elizabeth's face reddened slightly. "For your functions," she said, and I still had no idea what she was talking about.

"If we need to go to the bathroom," Ray whispered.

My face turned a bright red. No toilets in 1851? Gross. We disappeared into separate bedrooms and changed into the strange clothes. I'd worn a dress a few times in my life, usually for one of my uncle's board functions at Broward Academy, but nothing like this. The dress was long and stiff and difficult to squeeze into, and when I emerged from the bedroom, I felt ridiculous and could hardly move. Ray looked just as uncomfortable, tugging at his collar. The pants were a tad long, but otherwise the suit fit nicely.

"Much better," Elizabeth said, slapping her hands together. "You both look wonderful. Would you like me to go with you?"

I thought about that. Maybe she could help. At minimum, she could introduce us to Earlier Grandmother. But no, I didn't want to endanger her, too. And I suspected the longer we were here, the more dangerous it would become. There was also the matter of doing things that might change history. The fewer people involved, the better. "That's OK," I said. "We'll find her." Elizabeth smiled and pulled me into another hug. How wonderful that felt. For good measure, she hugged Ray, too. His eyes welled up and I knew he was thinking about his own mother. Two motherless children, crying for what we'd lost. I wiped my face and focused on the image of 1851

Noelle. I made the portal, gave Elizabeth a final wave, took Ray's hand, and we dove through.

Ray didn't vomit this time. But he did land on his head. So he wasn't too happy with me once he'd collected himself. Earlier Grandmother wasn't happy with me either, because people were screaming and fleeing every which way. I hadn't looked closely at what she was doing before I dove through the portal. That had been a mistake. She was in the middle of a small village, though I was still thoroughly confused by this. Hadn't Grandmother found the first Defender in New York City? And even more confusing, just about everyone was African American. I thought of the time we were in. This was before the Civil War. Before Abraham Lincoln freed the slaves. We were in New York, however, the North. So I guessed (hoped) all these black people were free.

Noelle walked up to us and screamed, "Who are you? What do you think you're doing jumping right into the middle of all this?"

"I-I-I'm Carol," I stuttered. Grandmother had never gotten that angry with me, and it caught me off guard. "This is Ray. I'm sorry."

"How did you do that?" she asked. "And where did you get that?" She pointed to my cane.

I'm part elf, I said telepathically, and it had the usual effect. A look of shock passed across her face. "You gave me this cane," I said hurriedly. "You sent us here to help you. From the future." Noelle seemed to be working this out in her head. The shimmering elf had already been kicked out of the elf kingdom at this point in history, so she knew time travel was possible. But it was still a lot to swallow. "You're in horrible danger," I added.

"What do you mean? From whom?"

"You're looking for someone, right? Someone with power?"

"How do you know that?"

"How do you think?" I asked, and understanding flitted across her face. "Someone is coming to try and stop you."

"From what?"

"Finding the person you're looking for. We think he wants to destroy that person."

The elf looked at Ray, studying him up and down. "What do you have to say for yourself? And why are you wearing my husband's suit?"

He looked down at his clothes. "Elizabeth gave them to me."

"She helped us find you," I said.

Noelle rolled her eyes. "That silly girl. Always so trusting." She reached out and touched my hair. "You both have the mark. It means something, doesn't it?"

"Yes," I answered. "But I can't tell you more."

"Oh really," the elf said. "So how do I know you're who you say you are? Why should I trust you?"

"Oh, wait, you told us to tell you something," I said. "Santa forgives you for what you did."

The elf gasped and stepped back. "You couldn't possibly . . . I told no one."

"I don't know what it means," I added hurriedly. "Grand . . . future you said you'd understand." The elf raised an eyebrow. I hoped she hadn't caught what I almost let slip. I had to be more careful. It was like handling a bottle of nitroglycerine. Make a wrong move and everything could explode. "We just want to help," I said.

"Something terrible is about to happen and we're here to stop it."

The elf thought about this for what seemed like forever. The three of us were alone now, the village quiet, everyone hiding. I wondered how many eyes watched us. She finally looked at me and nodded. "Alright. Let's find this mystery person. But if I suspect you of doing anything that gets in my way, you'll rue the day. Understand?" Ray and I nodded dumbly. And through the village she strode, Ray and I close behind.

He sat alone at the edge of the village, his head bent and the steam rising from his mouth with every breath in the frigid air. He wore no coat, and when he sat up at the sound of our approach, the telltale red hair with the white stripe became readily apparent. If I hadn't been accustomed to Defenders of all colors having the red hair, he might have struck me as peculiar looking. A black person with red hair was quite unusual. That, it turned out, was part of the reason he was alone.

The boy stood and turned to us. He looked scared. "Who are you?" he barked. He sounded scared, too. His fingers flexed at his sides and I wondered if he'd discovered his power yet. That, too, turned out to be part of the reason he was alone.

"We're friends," Noelle said, stopping several feet from the boy. She held out her hand to make sure we stopped behind her.

"No white people ever been my friends." He flicked a curious glance at Ray, who clearly was not "white people."

"Why are you out here alone?" I asked. Noelle shot me a warning glare. The boy's shoulders twitched. He was tall and skinny, probably a couple of years older than Ray and I, but it was difficult to tell because he had the face of a young child, wide-eyed and babyish. He had round cheeks and his ears stuck out a bit too far. His clothes were little more than rags and the only reason he wasn't shivering had to be because of the Defender power he possessed. The boy frowned at me with his baby face and I almost smiled. He reminded me of a little kid who's furious about something while everyone around him just thinks he's being adorable.

"Been alone for a long time," the boy said, and his face seemed to age ten years. His voice began to rise. "And now that I lost her, I'll be alone forever." He rocked back and forth. He breathed hard through his nose. Something was making him angry, or sad, or both. Noelle moved back. But I felt sorry for the boy. I wanted to give him a hug. I stepped forward. The boy's eyes grew wider. I took another step forward, holding out my hands, and he moved back. *No, Carol,* Noelle warned. *No!*

But it was too late. As I took my next step, the boy rocked from side to side even faster, harder, like he was powering up. I realized it with only a moment to spare. If I hadn't put up my cane to deflect the blast, we might have gotten hurt bad, maybe killed. As it was, the pulse blew the three of us backward. The next thing I knew, Noelle was shaking me awake. I had no idea how long we'd been out, but we were lying twenty feet from where we'd been standing and it was dark. The boy was gone.

"I'm sorry," I said to Noelle, who looked more than a little annoyed.

"You need to listen to what I say," she snapped, rubbing the back of her head and wincing. "If you're not from this world, then you don't know how it works."

"Why was he so scared?" I asked. "We weren't going to hurt him."

"He's an escaped slave," Noelle said solemnly. "He trusts no one."

It was as if she had grabbed my beating heart and squeezed. I couldn't breathe. I wanted to say I was sorry again, but I couldn't speak either. This kid, not much older than I was, had been owned by someone, forced to work, probably separated from his family. I finally managed to whisper, "I'm sorry."

"I wouldn't trust anyone either," Noelle said.

I wondered if people were chasing him. No wonder he was scared. "Should we try to find him again?"

"Let him be for a bit," Noelle said. "Something must have upset him before we arrived. I've been watching him for a while now and when he gets worked up like that, he can't control the power he has."

I glanced at Ray and he looked away. We both knew exactly what the boy was dealing with. How terrible for him not to have someone like Mr. Winters to guide him. "OK," I said softly.

"Are you kids hungry?" Noelle asked.

"Yes!" Ray and I said in unison. I realized the last thing we'd eaten were the cold beans and peanut butter sandwiches in the abandoned subway station.

"Come on then," Noelle said. "A friend of mine runs a place nearby and is up on all of the comings and goings. Maybe we can learn more about our powerful young friend. You're in for a treat. Elijah's quite the character."

CHAPTER 9

Seneca Village

"What is this place?" I asked. "Where is it?" We walked through a country town with thirty to forty houses, a church, a school, a general store, and a building with a hanging sign advertising the Red Dragon.

"Seneca Village," Noelle said.

My ears perked up at that name. That's where the Ancient One said Santa would come to find her and the first Defender. I couldn't wait to see the Big Guy! "I thought we were in New York City," I said.

"Seneca Village is above the city. Negroes settled here and bought the land." I knew from my history classes that *negro* was a common term of the day to describe black people. "Some Irish have moved in, too," Noelle continued. "Escaping famine in their homeland." A black and Irish village in New York in the 1850s? Soooooo cool. I had no idea such a place ever existed.

We entered the Red Dragon, which was filled with patrons eating and drinking and talking loudly around about a dozen small tables. Gas lamps hung on the walls and candles burned on every table, giving the room a warm glow. Whatever was being served smelled amazing, and my stomach gurgled. When we walked in, the room fell silent. I quickly realized why. Noelle and I were the only white people/elves in the entire place. I waved shyly, but everyone just stared. All except for a little girl, maybe four or five, who waved back enthusiastically. She had big round eyes and was so cute she looked like a doll Santa might leave under someone's tree. But everyone else was stone-faced and I rocked forward and back uncomfortably.

"Noelle!" a man shouted from behind the bar. He leaped over and ran toward us, a smile stretching from ear to ear. He was enormous, tall and broad-shouldered, muscles rippling on top of other muscles. His bald head shone like a Christmas ball hanging from a tree, and he wore plain gray overalls that looked a little like the uniforms people wore in Uncle Christopher's world. A dirty white apron was tied around his waist. The man embraced Noelle, lifting the tiny elf right off of her feet. I couldn't help but laugh, and everyone in the room went back to eating and drinking and talking.

"Carol, Ray," Noelle said, "I would like to introduce Elijah, the owner of this fine establishment."

Elijah beamed and pulled us into a hug. He nearly squeezed the life out of us, jamming us together so that we wound up cheek to cheek. I pulled away from Ray, both of us red-faced. "Any friend of Noelle's is a friend of mine," he said, practically shouting. "Welcome to the Red Dragon!" He nudged us toward an open table. "And Merry Christmas!" A small tree near the bar had been decorated simply with red ribbons, pinecones, and topped with a star made out of sticks.

Ray mumbled, "Merry Christmas," glancing nervously at our surroundings.

"Merry Christmas," I said. "How do you know my . . ." Noelle glanced curiously at me again. "Noelle?" I finished.

"I worked as a livery driver downtown," Elijah said. "She was my most loyal customer, and a good tipper. She helped me save for this place." He beamed with pride. I could see why. The tavern was warm and cozy, everything neat and orderly, with plenty of customers. "What can I get you? The rabbit is excellent."

I tried not to cringe at the thought of eating bunnies. I didn't want to offend Elijah. Not to mention the fact that I was starving. "That sounds good," I said. Ray and Noelle nodded. And ten minutes later, we each had a plate full of rabbit, potatoes, and freshly baked bread. The aromas were so wonderful they made me lightheaded.

Elijah sat in an empty chair, which groaned under his humongousness. Another patron motioned repeatedly to our cheerful new friend, but Elijah ignored him. "So what can I do for you?" he asked.

Noelle glanced at the other customers. She leaned close to Elijah. "Tell us about the boy with the red hair."

Elijah's brow crinkled, the furrows of his massive forehead like valleys between great mountains. For the first time since we'd met, his smile vanished. "The devil child," he said softly. "That's what they call him."

"He's not a devil," I said indignantly.

Elijah raised an eyebrow, making half valleys. "Yes, child. I know he's not a devil. I've been taking food out to him. But there is something strange about him. He frightens people."

"We want to help him," Noelle said. "Do you know where he stays?"

"Out in the forest. I took him blankets just yesterday. It was the strangest thing." Elijah hesitated.

"What?" Ray asked. He leaned into Elijah's every word.

"The trees around him were knocked down, as if a giant had felled them."

Ray and I looked at each other. We knew what that meant. The boy must be truly powerful if he was knocking down trees with no knowledge of how to focus his ability.

"Show us," Noelle said.

Elijah nodded and his smile reappeared, as broad as ever. "Right after closing time. Enjoy your meals." And he returned to work, finally fetching a new drink for his frustrated customer.

Elijah put us in front of the crackling fire and I enjoyed the next couple of hours relaxing and chatting with Noelle. Seeing her younger and stronger was soooooo cool, but it was frustrating having to be so careful what I said. She wanted to know more about the future, of course. "We can't," I said. "Future you said we should say as little as possible or it could mess things up."

She didn't press us further. But Ray, who'd spent most of the time staring at the fire, whispered, "It's a terrible place to live." I started to stop him, but the tears in his eyes paralyzed my tongue. And maybe *his* future was OK to talk about since we hoped to change it anyway. "People like us are hunted. We live like animals with barely enough to eat, and an evil dictator monitors our every move."

"That's why we're here, Ray," I said, touching his shoulder. "We're going to fix that."

He stared grimly into the flickering flames. "Yeah, about that. I've been thinking. What if when we change things, something big in my life changes? Maybe my mom is never born in your reality. Which would mean I cease to exist."

I had wondered the same thing and had no answer for him. I kept thinking of my father and whether he existed in the world my uncle created. But Mr. Winters did, even if it was a different version of Mr. Winters. And so did Toby Wise, the Defender I'd known. That led me to believe Dad existed here, and Ray and his mom would exist in my world, too. "I think she'll be there, and hopefully you'll be together again." Ray nodded, looking away so I wouldn't see the tears in his eyes. I felt so sorry for him. I turned to Noelle. "I won't say too much about my world, except that Christmas is a magical, wonderful time, and some evil person changed all of that."

"Magical?" Noelle asked. "You're talking about Santa?"

I nodded, deciding it was OK to confirm guesses she had about the future. She grimaced, which seemed odd. "What's wrong?" I asked.

She looked away. "Nothing."

"Come on," I said. "I can tell it's not nothing."

She sighed and asked, "Santa brings toys to every child on Christmas?"

I nodded.

"And the elves help make them?"

"Of course," I said.

"So his vision came true," she said. "No thanks to me."

"What do you mean?" I asked.

She hung her head. "Santa asked for my help. He asked me to persuade the other elves to join him."

"They haven't always worked for Santa?" Ray asked.

Noelle sniffed. "Hardly. elves are a prickly bunch. Very independent. We weren't crazy about him moving so close to our realm in the first place."

"Where did he come from?" Ray asked.

"No one knows for sure and he won't say," Noelle said. "But I liked him from the beginning and we became friends. He told me about his dream. He wanted to bring toys to every good boy and girl in the world. He had already started small, giving toys where he could. But he needed elves to go bigger. He asked me to help persuade the others to help." She hesitated.

"What happened?" Ray asked.

"I was selfish," she said. "I wanted to see the world. I didn't want to be stuck in the North Pole making toys. So I told Santa he was on his own and I left."

"You wanted your own life," I said. "Santa probably understood that."

"I was a leader. Someone destined to rule the elf world. So when I took off, the other elves didn't cooperate with Santa. And before I left, Santa and I had an argument. I said terrible things."

"What?" I asked, hardly breathing. I couldn't even conceive of Santa and Grandmother exchanging a harsh word.

Noelle sat back in her chair and stared at the ceiling. "That he was a silly old man wasting his time on a crazy dream. Toys for the entire world!" She sniffed again. "Impossible." I cringed, imagining how those words must have hurt Santa. "He told me he might have a way, but he needed my help."

"You didn't believe him?" Ray asked.

"Would you?" Noelle asked. "The other elves heard our argument and decided that if I was going to live my own life, why shouldn't they?"

"So none of them helped?" I asked.

"A few. But not enough." She shook her head. "He must have succeeded, though, right? Despite what I did?" She looked at me hopefully.

I squirmed, wishing I could tell her about the Defenders and the elves and the magical world of Christmas that I knew. "You know I can't say," I said. "It's too dangerous. But Santa forgives you. Your future self told me to tell you that."

Noelle smiled. "I hope so." Then her eyes lit up. "Wait, does all this have something to do with the boy, with Santa's plan?" I squirmed again, looking away. "I know, I know," she said. "You can't say."

After that, we sat quietly for a long while waiting for Elijah to finish. My eyelids grew heavy, but I didn't want to sleep, afraid of missing something important. I noticed a newspaper on the table next to Noelle. *Can I see?* I asked telepathically.

She handed me the newspaper, which was considerably different from the ones in my world. The paper was only a few pages thick but almost cloth-like, much sturdier than modern newspapers and filled with rows of tiny gray type. "*The Liberator*," I read aloud.

"An abolitionist newspaper," Noelle said. I searched my memory bank. I knew that word, but history wasn't my strong suit. Noelle looked at my blank expression. "Anti-slavery," she said.

Then I remembered. Before the Civil War, preachers, politicians, newspaper editors, and other activists spoke out on the evils of slavery. They would eventually win, but not before the country was ripped apart and thousands upon thousands died in the Civil War. I thought of Frederick Douglass, one of the black activists we had studied at Broward Academy. He was a slave who escaped, learned to read, and became a great statesman. Too bad we couldn't look him up in 1851. It would be so cool to talk with a historical figure I'd read about in my textbooks.

I looked at the front page of *The Liberator*. At the top above the name was an illustration of a slave sale. An auctioneer shouted out prices as black people cowered beneath him. And below was the quote: "Our Country Is the World – Our Countrymen Are Mankind."

"What does that mean?" I asked Noelle, pointing to the quote.

She studied it. "That's Mr. Garrison's philosophy."

"Who?"

"William Lloyd Garrison, the abolitionist. He thinks our country should be leading the world, setting an example of freedom. But we keep our countrymen, the negro, in chains."

I thought of the poor "devil child," as the townspeople called him, and how he had escaped those very chains. I fell asleep wondering what awful things he had endured in his short life.

Noelle shook me awake in what seemed like the blink of an eye. The Red Dragon was empty and Elijah was shoving his last customer out the door, a fellow who'd had so much of the Red Dragon's "special ale" he could barely walk. Elijah untied his apron, blew out all the candles, turned off the gas lamps, and motioned for us to follow him into the Seneca Village night.

The streets were barren. A lone lamppost flickered weakly and cast long shadows that moved as if they were alive. I wished we could use Ray's flashlight but figured Elijah would safely lead us where we needed to go. He carried a small lantern and we trudged silently past the last house of the village, following a dirt trail into the dark woods. It still blew my mind that this was New York City. We were in the countryside! And night creatures scurried and hooted and chattered, stopping only at our approach. Stumbling through the woods, I nearly fell and Ray caught me before I went down. I smiled at him, embarrassed.

Elijah motioned for us to stop. "Let me go ahead. He knows me." He disappeared, his lantern fading into the night. We stood in almost pitch-black. Something slithered through the brush and I shuddered. We heard Elijah calling softly for the boy. I spotted a glimmer of the lantern among the trees, but there was no answer. And when Elijah returned a few minutes later, I wasn't surprised when he told us, "He's gone."

"Where?" I asked, feeling dumb the moment I said it.

He shrugged. "Still running. Easy to understand why considering how the townfolk treated him."

Noelle looked unconvinced and glanced at me as Elijah held up his lantern and peered into the woods. *Make a portal without drawing attention to yourself,* she said. *Find him.* She walked over to Elijah, saying, "I think I saw something move." While our guide was turned the other direction,

I concentrated on the brief glimpse I'd gotten of the boy, zeroing in on his baby face. The portal crackled before me. The picture came into focus. And I was confused. The boy lay on what looked like a hospital bed. His eyes were closed. I couldn't tell if he was sleeping or something more ominous. He appeared to be alone.

Noelle glanced at me and I nodded. *I found him.*

"Thank you for trying, Elijah," Noelle said. "I guess he's gone. We'll let you return to the Red Dragon."

"You'll be all right?" he asked. "I can put you up for the night."

"No need," Noelle said. "A carriage awaits to take us home. Though my driver can't compare to you."

Elijah gave us a glorious smile and embraced Noelle again, lifting her off the ground. He gave Ray and me a farewell bear hug and ambled back down the path toward Seneca Village. We waited until we could no longer hear him, then Noelle said, "These powers you have, tell me about them."

"We can do what the boy does, blasting things with invisible waves of energy," I said. "Plus, I can stop time. I freeze everything and everybody."

Noelle raised her eyebrows. "Remarkable." She rubbed her chin, lost in thought. "Use your powers and we will go to the boy. Freeze him so he doesn't attack us again."

I nodded and took a deep breath. My heart thumped as I concentrated on him. I needed a larger portal for the three of us, so I used my cane to focus the energy. The portal sizzled with the cane's power. It was almost my height, maybe the best one I'd ever made, and Noelle and I each took one of Ray's hands. "One, two, three!" I said, and we jumped.

We landed in the hospital room across from the boy. I raised my hand to freeze time, delayed momentarily while I steadied myself. But before I could, a massive blast of energy knocked me off of my feet. The breath rushed from my chest. Ray and Noelle flew through the air. I landed across the room. My head snapped back, smacking the hard floor. And I saw nothing but blackness.

I awoke to the sight of Uncle Christopher's face only a foot from mine, and for a moment, I thought I was back home in Hillsboro in his mansion. He was waking me for school, the one household task he never left to a member of his staff. "Up, Carol!" he would say every morning, an edge to his voice. He was always so impatient, as if I annoyed him simply by sleeping. But strangely enough, I cherished those moments. He was the only family I had at the time. And I believed that underneath his gruff manner, he truly did care for me. Why else would he wake me himself?

"Up, Carol!" That edge. That impatience. I opened my eyes, almost expecting to be in my old bed, surrounded by my collection of fifty-nine Santas, my Christmas lights glowing, the tree shimmering. But none of it was there. Just Uncle Christopher.

He was skinnier and looked even more chiseled from stone than he did when I lived with him. I wondered vaguely if he were sick. I felt a tinge of worry. But I slapped that away, angry with myself. Why should I care about that after all he'd done? I answered my own question, arguing with myself. Because I'm human. Not evil. And he's my family, like it or not. "Up, Carol," he repeated. And this time it wasn't impatience. It was disgust, as if I repulsed him.

"Where am I?" I mumbled, then realized I couldn't move. My hands were secured by leather straps. I was in an old bed, still wearing my 1851 dress. Noelle, Ray, and the boy were in separate beds, all motionless. We were in that hospital room, Noelle and Ray also strapped in. Light streamed through two high windows, which meant we'd been out cold all night. The boy wasn't strapped in, which surprised me. And why wasn't he dead? Isn't that why my uncle came back? To destroy the first Defender? To keep Santa from forming the group that would help him deliver toys and protect him?

"You're just where I want you to be," Uncle Christopher said and he pulled back, his lip curled in a snarl. I yanked at my straps. I concentrated on trying to freeze him. But I spotted the machine, just like the ones that blocked our power in his world. He must have brought it from the future. I was helpless. Trapped.

"What are you going to do with me?" I asked. "With us?"

"Oh, I have big plans for you all," Uncle Christopher said. He carried a staff, similar to the one he'd used in our Christmas Eve battle over the mountains of West Virginia. Only this one glowed and pulsed more powerfully, a deeper, uglier shade of green. Like the color of radioactive slime.

"You're going to kill us," I said as the reality of our situation sank in. So this was how I would be defeated, how I would die. I'd failed Grandmother, Ray, Mr. Winters, Dad, Santa. I'd failed the entire world.

Uncle Christopher placed his hand over his heart, as if he were aghast at the very idea he would harm us. "You think so lowly of me, Carol," he said and smiled. A chill crept along my spine, as if it had been hiding under me on the bed and was trying to escape. "No, I won't kill you. In fact, I plan on reuniting you with your dear father. You are family, after all. And one must always take care of family."

"What do you mean?" I shouted. "What did you do with him?" Noelle's eyes popped open and she looked around wildly, yanking at the straps that tied her down.

Uncle Christopher paid her no mind. "Let's just say that time will be on your side. You might even live forever. That will be my final gift to you. Eternity." And he laughed cruelly.

I was hopelessly confused. My uncle was never the type to show mercy. I saw it in how ruthlessly he ran his toy empire, crushing rival companies and buying up smaller toy makers to absorb into International Toy. I saw it when he blasted Ramon out of the sky over the Dominican Republic. And again when he did the same to Santa and the Defenders and tried to do it to me. His heart was stone. The world he ruled with fear showed that. I couldn't imagine him ever offering me a "gift."

Noelle couldn't either. Even though this version of Grandmother knew nothing about my uncle, she saw right through him. "You found them, didn't you?" she asked, barely more than a whisper.

That confused me even more. "Who?" Grandmother always seemed to be two steps ahead of me, and her younger self was no different.

"The missing elves."

"I don't understand."

"Ah, dearest niece, you never were all that quick, were you?" my uncle said. "Never one to apply yourself in your studies." I cringed, remembering how I struggled at Brower Academy. My uncle walked over to Noelle's bed. "I don't believe we've had the pleasure. Christopher Glover at your service." He bowed, mocking the helpless elf.

"Noelle," she said. "Charmed, I'm sure."

"Who did he find?" I asked impatiently.

"The elf's wife and son," Noelle said. "Your uncle figured it out."

Then the pieces of the puzzle fell into place. He had actually found the elf's family. And if he knew where they were, that meant he knew how to get there. And that also meant he knew how to send other people there. "Dad," I said softly.

"Ah, now you're catching on, Carol," Uncle Christopher said. "Good girl."

"You put him there?" I asked, horrified.

"That foolish elf thinks he's the expert on time travel. But it didn't take me long to master. It requires discipline, Carol, something you've always lacked. You get that from your father."

"Bring him back right now!" I screamed. Ray began to stir, moaning softly.

"And why would I do that?" Uncle Christopher asked. "Your father is weak. He wasted his gift protecting that silly old man and his toys. We have this ability for a reason. And that's to rule, to shape the world as we see fit. Which is exactly what I did. And why I came back to this dreadful time and place."

"To destroy the first Defender?" I asked.

My uncle gasped, clutching his chest as if I'd wounded him. "Again, Carol dear. You think so poorly of me. I didn't come back to destroy anybody. I came back to awaken him and set him on the right path."

"I don't understand."

My uncle smiled. "Before I give you my final gift, I'm going to show you. So when you join your father, you can ponder how easily human beings are swayed. Santa would have misused this poor boy's talents." My uncle touched the captured boy's forehead gently, unfreezing him. "Time for the show, dear."

The boy bolted upright in his bed, his eyes flaring with fear. Uncle Christopher stepped back and held out his hands to calm him. I started to yell, "Don't listen—" but my uncle waved his hand and froze me.

The boy looked around the room, his gaze stopping on each of us. "Who are you?" he asked my uncle. "And them?"

"The enemy, Sebwe," Uncle Christopher whispered, his eyes wide in mock fear. He leaned in close to the boy. "They want to destroy you." I wanted to scream at his lies, to fling a pulse at my uncle and blow him into oblivion.

The boy's eyes narrowed. "Why would they do that?" He studied us, his curious gaze lingering on Noelle. "How do you know my name?"

"I know all about you, Sebwe," Uncle Christopher answered. "I want to help you."

"No white man ever wanted to help me."

"Then I, Christopher Glover, shall be the first." My uncle bowed grandly, not mockingly this time. He had summoned the charming and sincere version of himself, the one he used for business clients or the Brower Academy school board.

"How?"

"Your mother," Uncle Christopher said.

The boy's eyes went round and he stood, bristling with intensity and power. My uncle didn't move; he had no reason to fear this child with his raw, untapped ability. "What about her?" Sebwe asked.

"You lost her, didn't you?" Uncle Christopher said. "You escaped because of the power within you, but you were separated from her."

Tears spilled down the boy's cheeks. He hung his head. "Yes," he answered.

"I'll show you how to use that power. I have it, too, Sebwe." The boy looked up in surprise and Uncle Christopher nodded. "We'll find her together. And we won't let these evil people . . ." He motioned toward us. ". . . destroy you."

I felt like I was going to explode. Lie after lie after lie, and the boy was swallowing it all.

"How?" Sebwe asked.

"You need to help me. I need you to picture your mother. Think about her face, every detail of what she looks like. Then take my hand." He reached out to Sebwe. "What's her name?"

The boy hesitated. I tried to signal him with my eyes, a raised eyebrow, anything. But I was concrete. "Ruth," Sebwe said. "I'm afraid she got recaptured."

"We'll find her," Uncle Christopher said. "Concentrate on her." The boy closed his eyes and gave Uncle Christopher his hand. My uncle closed his eyes, too. Sweat beaded on his forehead. He opened his eyes and made a circle with his hands. The air crackled. A portal formed. A woman appeared, hiding in the woods, eyes wide with terror. "Open your eyes," Uncle Christopher said. "Take my staff. Let the energy flow through you and the portal will be revealed."

Sebwe studied the staff, his brow wrinkled in doubt. It seemed Uncle Christopher had grown even more powerful since his escape. I'd never seen anyone use another person to make a portal to find someone. The boy took the staff. Energy coursed through him. He cried out. Then his eyes focused on the portal, the hiding woman. "Mama!" He reached out to her but my uncle gently blocked his hand.

"Not yet," he said. "We'll get her if you promise to help me."

Sebwe stared longingly at his mom and I ached for him. It wasn't fair what my uncle was doing, using his mom to manipulate the boy. "Promise what?" he asked.

"Come work for me and avoid the ordinary fate that's in store for you. You are anything but ordinary, my child, and I will help you reach your potential."

The boy glanced from his mother to my uncle and back to his mother again. "You don't make sense," he said. "But if you get me my mama, I'll do whatever you want."

My uncle rested his hand on the boy's shoulder. "You won't regret this, Sebwe."

Uncle Christopher pulled the boy by the arm and the two of them stepped into the portal. They vanished for a moment before reappearing in the forest.

The boy's mother screamed but then spotted her son and raced toward him, tears streaming down her cheeks. "My baby!"

"Mama!" the boy shouted, and the two of them embraced, the boy lifting his tiny mother off her feet. I hated what my uncle was doing, but the joy of their reunion swept through me, filling me with warmth. "Where did you come from?" Ruth asked.

"This man's gonna help us."

Uncle Christopher bowed. "Time to go, Sebwe," Uncle Christopher said.

"We leaving?" Ruth asked. My uncle nodded and she looked at him with suspicion. "How?" she asked.

Uncle Christopher didn't answer. He waved his staff through the air. The portal vanished.

A new portal opened seconds later and the three of them stepped through. Sebwe's mom screamed as they appeared instantly in our room. She looked around at us, confused. She breathed as if she'd run all the way from the forest. She turned to Uncle Christopher. "What's happening? Who are these people?"

"People trying to hurt me," Sebwe said. Ruth stared hard at me and I thought I saw a flash of something. Suspicion maybe. I hoped she could sense that my uncle couldn't be trusted. But perhaps that was wishful thinking. He had just reunited her with her son.

"Yes, yes," Uncle Christopher said impatiently. "Awful, awful people. Now that you're back with your mother, Sebwe, it's time for you to help me."

The boy nodded and Uncle Christopher grinned. "Excellent," he said. "This isn't quite like how I changed things before, but with you here, Carol, I think it'll be even more fun this time around. Let's get to work."

And with that horrible smile of his, I knew without a doubt that the world was doomed.

CHAPTER 10

The Defeat of Santa Claus

Ray and Noelle were turning purple, fighting for breath. So what choice did I have? My uncle stood over them, manipulating the air and space, squeezing and smothering, all while controlling me. He had grown so powerful since the last time I'd seen him, when I'd let him get away. I couldn't defeat him now. I was sure of it. And I couldn't stop what he was doing either, which is why I gave in and told him about Santa's arrival.

"When?" he shouted. I screamed when it looked like Noelle and Ray might stop breathing entirely.

"Soon! After sunset!" I yelled.

"Where?" he asked and squeezed even tighter. They groaned in agony. Sebwe and his mother watched in silence. Ruth flinched with every flick of my uncle's hand.

"Wherever Sebwe is. Santa senses him and goes to him. It was supposed to happen in Seneca Village. Please stop hurting them!"

Uncle Christopher smiled. "Of course, Carol dear." He waved his hand and Noelle and Ray gasped and coughed, their color slowly returning to normal. And I hated myself. Not only had I failed to stop my uncle, but I had also betrayed Santa.

Sebwe's mother got up and crossed the room. Uncle Christopher glanced at her in surprise. She went to a sink, pulled a bowl from the shelf, and filled it with water. She found a small rag, dropped it into the bowl, and carried it back to the three of us. She stopped next to Noelle's bed. Sebwe watched her with alarm. "What are you doing, Mama?" he whispered.

She lightly wrung out the rag and folded it into a rectangle, dabbing Noelle's forehead. The elf smiled up at her. "Seen enough of that sort of thing in my day," Ruth said. "Don't need to see more."

Uncle Christopher's face betrayed a hint of anger, but

he summoned his most charming smile. "You are right, madam. No need for such unpleasantness. One final task and Carol and her friends will be on their way. And you and Sebwe can live free. No one will ever control you again."

"And what are you doing?" Ruth asked. "Seems like you're doing plenty of controlling yourself."

"Mama!" Sebwe shouted. "He's helping us!"

Uncle Christopher didn't bother to hide his anger now. "Listen to your son. I can make other arrangements if you've had enough of my hospitality."

Ruth glared at him. She dropped the rag back into the water and went to Ray's bed. She dabbed his forehead and caressed his cheek. "Aren't you a handsome boy in your fine suit?"

Uncle Christopher watched her. Sebwe's eyes darted between him and his mama. Uncle Christopher forced another smile. "Fine, fine, you care for our guests."

He made a portal and the shimmering elf appeared on the other side. "Come, I need you," Uncle Christopher barked and the elf jumped as if someone had hollered "Boo!" He cast his eyes down at the sight of my uncle. He reminded me of a small wolf in one of those nature shows, cowering before the leader of the pack. "I know where your family is," Uncle Christopher said.

The elf's eyes came alive, the pack leader unexpectedly tossing the skinny wolf a bone. He nodded and the portal vanished. A new one appeared and the elf jumped through. Sebwe and his mother yelped at his appearance out of thin air. "Where are they?" the elf asked, moving in so close to Uncle Christopher that he shoved the elf to the ground. The elf shimmered to a child version of himself and I thought Ruth might faint. She gripped the edge of the bed.

"Patience!" Uncle Christopher snapped, looking at the elf with disgust. "I have one more task for you and then you shall be reunited with your family."

The elf's face fell. I wondered how long he'd been working with my uncle. Maybe he'd grown to mistrust his promises.

"It's time to have a chat with Santa," Uncle Christopher said. "Let's call it a business meeting." He laughed. "I need you to make a portal so my friends can watch our little meeting before I send them on their way."

"That's all?" the elf asked. "Then you'll bring me my family?"

"I will indeed." The elf shifted into an elderly version and my uncle's face scrunched in disgust again. "Though I do wonder what they'll think of you in your current state."

"I care nothing for that," the elf said. "I just want them safe."

"How noble. Truly an inspiration to us all." Uncle Christopher smirked and turned to his captives. "You three behave while we're gone. Since I won't be here to keep you quiet, I'll have to do it the old-fashioned way." He opened a drawer near the sink and took out an old towel stained brown and yellow. He tore it into long pieces and gagged each of us, tying the cloth tightly behind our heads. I retched at the smell. "Come, Sebwe," Uncle Christopher said and made a portal. I recognized the woods next to Seneca Village. He took Sebwe's hand and strolled through.

Sebwe's mother gasped as her son disappeared. She ran to where he'd vanished. "Sebwe? Sebwe? Where did he take my boy?"

"He'll be fine," the shimmering elf snapped. "Go back to your seat!" He closed his eyes in concentration, circled his hands, and a portal appeared. Uncle Christopher and Sebwe snuck along the edge of the forest near Seneca Village. They crouched behind bushes and waited.

Carol, Noelle said telepathically. Her voice made me jump and the elf glanced over. I wondered if he could "hear" us. I'd gotten pretty good at directing my telepathy to the elf I was talking to and no one else. Surely Noelle, a full-blooded elf, could speak to me without the shimmering elf knowing. *We need to persuade him to help us.* Her eyes motioned toward the elf.

How? I asked.

Talk with him, Noelle said. *He'll never listen to me.*

He won't listen to some girl he just met either, I argued.

You must try.

What could I possibly say to the elf? Nothing I'd done so far had worked in the slightest. If anything, my uncle was even happier now that he also had me in his clutches. But I concentrated on the shimmering elf. Uncle Christopher and Sebwe still hid behind the bushes. Sebwe looked terrified. There was no sign of Santa. *Sir*, I said to the elf.

He glanced at me with annoyance. *Quiet!*

No, I said, annoyed right back at him. He was a big jerk in a tiny package. *What you're doing is wrong and you know it.*

I don't care, he answered. *I have to get my family back.*

You think they'd want you helping someone take over the world just so they could be free? You've seen what he does. How cruel he is.

They can think what they want of me. I just want them free.

There has to be a better way. I have powers, too, you know. If you let us go, I'll help you. I promised your future self I would.

Do you know how to get to them? How to bring them back to me?

I didn't answer.

That's what I thought. Your dear uncle does. So whatever he asks, I'll do.

I'll figure it out, I said desperately. *I can do it, I swear.*

I can't take that chance. Now leave me alone. It's showtime.

Santa had appeared at the edge of the Seneca Village woods. He set his sleigh down softly. It was a small sleigh with only four reindeer, and he had no elves with him. He wasn't as big a deal in 1851, so maybe that's all he needed. But Santa looked pretty much the same, and my heart ached at the sight of him. His face was a bit younger looking, and he was skinnier, though his belly still shook under his red suit. I wondered if he'd already found Mrs. Claus. She'd be hard at work fattening him up to proper Santa proportions.

Santa's sleigh slid to a stop in an open spot near the woods. He scanned his surroundings, his eyebrows wrinkled in puzzlement. He hopped off of his sleigh and walked around to pet his reindeer, who nuzzled his furry cheek.

Uncle Christopher and Sebwe stepped from the shadows. Santa froze. Fear passed across his face like a ripple on a pond, but he collected himself quickly. "I suspected it might be you, Christopher," Santa said.

My uncle looked surprised. "So, you know who I am? What an honor."

"You don't think I've been watching you and your rogue elf?" Santa answered. "Messing around with time. Such bad, bad boys." He shook his head, adding a "Tsk. Tsk."

Uncle Christopher laughed. "I suppose that means I've made your Naughty List."

Santa just smiled. "And who do we have here?"

Uncle Christopher stepped between Sebwe and Santa. "That's none of your concern."

Santa peered around my uncle and said, "Oh, hello, Sebwe."

The boy jolted like he'd heard a gunshot. "How do you know me?"

"I know every boy and girl," Santa said warmly. He took a step toward Sebwe. "I know you've been through terrible things and that you're angry at the world. And I don't blame you for that." Sebwe's eyes filled with tears. "I know you want to protect your mother," Santa continued. "And you would do anything for her."

"Enough!" Uncle Christopher shouted. "Sebwe's with me now and he's going to be treated with the respect a boy of his talents deserves. Isn't that right, Sebwe?" Santa gave the boy the kindest of smiles. Santa knew (he always knows) what was in Sebwe's heart, how confused he was, how hard it was to know what to do. I held my breath, hoping Sebwe would rebel against my uncle, hoping he would choose Santa. But Sebwe nodded and Uncle Christopher snorted triumphantly.

Santa smiled again, a sad sort of smile. "Just take care of your mama, Sebwe, and know that you are loved."

My uncle sniffed. "Love is a waste of time. Power is what matters. And you're about to learn the full extent of *my* power." Uncle Christopher waved his hand through the air and aimed his staff at Santa's tiny sleigh. He blew it to pieces with a North Pulse, shards of wood raining down on the forest. The reindeer squealed and took off into the night sky. Santa stood alone. He remained calm, never betraying the fear I'm sure he was feeling. My uncle waved his hand again, manipulating the air so that Santa was lifted off of his feet. With his staff, Uncle Christopher created a portal, grabbed Sebwe by the arm, and pulled the two of them through. They materialized before us in the hospital. Santa landed hard, crashing shoulder first to the floor. He groaned when he looked up at the three of us strapped to our beds.

"Your rescuers," Uncle Christopher proclaimed. "And now that they know they've been defeated, I'll be sending them on their way. Then Sebwe and I will see what we can do about that elf kingdom. You can join us for that, Santa."

Uncle Christopher took the gags from our mouths, untying mine last. "What is wrong with you?" I shouted. "Why are you so evil?"

Uncle Christopher seemed taken aback. He studied me, as if trying to figure out a puzzle. "I'm not evil, Carol dear. I'm victorious. As I've told you before, life is competition. Survival. The strongest come out on top. That's how nature intended it."

"It doesn't have to be that way," I said. "What you're doing will cause so much pain."

"I lost my parents because of you," Ray said.

Uncle Christopher looked closely at Ray, his eyebrows lifting with recognition. "Ah, yes. I remember you now. The little White Stripe who slipped through our fingers." My uncle grinned. "Your mother says hello, by the way."

Ray's face went pale. "What did you do to her?!"

"The better question is what will we do with her now. Since we have you, she's no longer of any use to us."

"Don't you touch her!" Ray screamed.

Uncle Christopher waved his hand to silence him. "This is what happens when you don't cooperate. Your parents and Santa would waste your gift. We're meant for bigger things than delivering silly toys."

"That's where you're wrong, Christopher," Santa said. "It's not toys we deliver. It's joy. For all your power, that's what you lack."

"I lack nothing!" Uncle Christopher shouted. "And I've had enough of this conversation." He waved his staff and directed his hand toward us. The straps that held us snapped. He lifted us in the air. Sebwe and his mother watched in silence, their mouths hanging open. The shimmering elf smiled sadistically. Uncle Christopher spun us around and upright. I struggled against him, but my arms were pinned to my sides. He took his staff and closed his eyes, drawing power from the threads of time and space. He let go of his staff and it floated in front of him, turning slowly. What the shimmering elf had done with his machine, my uncle was doing with his staff, using it to amplify his own powers. The staff spun faster and faster. Beads of sweat popped out on Uncle Christopher's forehead. His body trembled. He circled his hand again and again. A portal opened, normal looking at first. But it slowly turned into a spinning vortex, as if we were looking down into a tornado. Uncle Christopher drilled deeper, further into time. He breathed hard. Sweat soaked his shirt. His eyes popped open and he smiled. "I found them."

The shimmering elf leaped forward, tripping over his own feet and nearly stumbling into the vortex. "Fool!" my uncle snapped.

"Please get them," the elf said. "I'm begging you."

Uncle Christopher sneered but refocused on the vortex, which spun and spun. He held out his hand and closed his eyes. He maneuvered his hand from side to side, forward and back, as if he were a magician performing a trick for a rapt audience. The elf leaned toward the vortex. Uncle Christopher's shirt was drenched. He grimaced and grunted and gave a huge yank. Out of the vortex came two elves, a beautiful woman and a young boy. I recognized them from the ice sculpture in the future elf's mansion.

The elf shrieked with joy and pulled his wife and child into a ferocious embrace. I couldn't help it, I felt happy for him, despite everything he'd done. I wondered how far I would go to save the ones I loved. And the two elves who had been lost were not to blame. I was glad they'd been rescued.

They looked dazed, as if they'd been awakened from a deep sleep, like a couple of Rip Van Winkles, only ones who had not aged. It took them a minute to orient themselves, and when they did, they hugged the shimmering elf as fiercely as he did them. He shifted to a young elf, almost as young as his son, and his wife stepped back in alarm. "What happened to you?"

He hung his head. "I've been searching for you for hundreds of years."

His wife gasped. "What time is this?"

"It's 1851," the elf said. "But my future self, the one who initiated the search, lives in 2019. He will want to see you."

"He will, you fool," Uncle Christopher interrupted. "She exists in this time now, which means she'll exist in the future."

My head spun, trying to grasp that. So if she existed now, she would be 168 years older in the future? But what if she and the child traveled to the future with my uncle? Would she cease to exist from 1851 to 2019? That would mean the past versions of the elf would once again lose her. It was all so confusing.

The shimmering elf also looked perplexed, but he seemed to figure it out. His expression turned to relief. "Then they will remain with me," he pronounced. "I'm not losing them again."

"Yes, yes, do what you wish," Uncle Christopher said. "I have more pressing matters." His face was alive with something now. I can't even describe it. Evil, joy, satisfaction, everything mixed into one horrible expression.

I felt fear like I'd never known. And helplessness. "What are you going to do?"

"I told you, Carol dear. I'm going to reunite you with your father." He glanced toward the spinning vortex. "Maybe someday, if I'm feeling nostalgic, I'll take you both out and we can have a family picnic. Hot dogs, corn on the cob, macaroni, wouldn't that be delightful?"

"Wait, what are you doing?" the shimmering elf's wife asked.

"None of your concern," Uncle Christopher snapped.

"Shhh," the shimmering elf hissed, looking terrified.

"He's sending us to where you just came from," Noelle said to the wife. "What's in there?"

"Quiet!" Uncle Christopher yelled.

"Confusion," the beautiful elf said. She seemed not to fear my uncle. Perhaps after what she'd been through, there was nothing left to fear. "Madness. And there are others in there."

"Dad!" I said. He had to be one of them. I wondered who else had been banished to the vortex. Mr. Winters? Ivan-I-Am-Not?

"Enough!" Uncle Christopher shouted. He waved his hand and everyone froze in place. Terror sparked in the elves' eyes, but none of them could move. "Time to go, Carol dear," Uncle Christopher said. His tone was almost tender. He leaned in and kissed me on the cheek. "I would have given you everything. You could have ruled the world after me. Such a terrible waste." He pulled away and gave me a final look, one filled with disdain. He waved his hand and Ray, Noelle, and I were flung into the vortex. I grabbed for them at the last moment, taking each by a hand, holding on as if my life depended on it. And we fell and fell.

Into confusion.

Into madness.

CHAPTER 11

Lost in Time

I watched a thousand years go by. Or a thousand seconds, or minutes, or days. It was impossible to tell.

"Daddy!" I screamed. His face flashed before me, an older version, bitter and defeated by what his brother had done. He saw me, too. Though there was no sign in his eyes that he recognized his own daughter. His mouth moved, but I heard nothing. Then he was gone, swirling in the vortex. "Grandmother!" I shouted. "Ray!" But my mouth made no sound and no answer came. I couldn't see them, even though I felt them, holding tightly to their hands. *Grandmother*, I repeated telepathically. *Noelle, are you there?* No answer. I was screaming into a void.

History flashed before me. The future, too. Histories and futures of those I knew or had seen.

Sebwe and Uncle Christopher destroying the elf kingdom. The ice structures crumbling. The great tree splintered by North Pulse after North Pulse. Santa collapsing in grief. Sebwe transforming, power and anger consuming his soul. Taking revenge on the world that had abused him. I saw his history, too. I watched his escape, when the power within him broke loose and he and Ruth fled, the two of them getting separated in the chaos. I saw the terrible guilt that weighed on him, the agony of wondering what was happening to the mother he so loved, and I understood him.

I watched Sebwe's mother, too. She wept as her son came under my uncle's sway, doing his evil bidding and getting rewarded for it. The son she knew, that sweet boy, vanished. She withdrew into herself, even though Sebwe became powerful and wealthy beyond imagining after my uncle returned to his time. Sebwe tried to coax her into his world, but she refused to speak to him. The life seemed to leave her and her remaining days were filled with sadness and disappointment. I mourned with her for the life she might have led. If Sebwe had become the first Defender like he was supposed to, surely Santa would have made their existences happy and fulfilling. I understood her pain.

Uncle Christopher bounced through time. Alliances were made. Armies marched. Battles were waged and won. No one was able to defeat him and his power. He built his empire through fear. He found others like him. They either bowed to him or they were destroyed or banished to the void. People who would have been Defenders, who would have spent their lives helping Santa Claus, instead became monsters like the man who led them. The White Stripes ruled. Humanity bent its knee. All thought that didn't conform to my uncle's view of the world was eliminated. In their depressing gray uniforms and terrifying lives, people became cogs in a giant machine controlled by Uncle Christopher. His philosophy had triumphed. The strongest came out on top. But I would never understand him. EVER.

Santa retreated, a broken man. My uncle kept him alive. Sadistic and cruel, he was like a cat toying with its prey. Santa tried sneaking away the year after the elf kingdom was destroyed, tried to visit homes on Christmas Eve and deliver a few toys to kids who really needed them. But my uncle was watching and waiting. He put a stop to that. Forever. No more visits from Santa. No more toys under the tree unless they came from one of Uncle Christopher's factories. Christmas lost all of its magic with no Santa, existing merely to enrich my evil uncle. Santa Claus, the one who would have delivered so much joy to the world, lived out his years in a home that became a prison. All alone. Nobody home.

The elves vanished, scattered to the winds, remnants of their kingdom disintegrating with time. They went into exile. Some fled to the ancient elven forest Grandmother had once explored. Others blended into the human population, trying to hide in plain sight. Uncle Christopher's minions tracked them down, one by one, until only a few remained.

Mr. Winters appeared, versions of him. Fighting, always fighting. Living on the run, trying to recruit others. Fleeing underground. Captured and tortured. My uncle always victorious. I even saw my mother and father at one point, revisiting her brief existence. That, at least, was a gift, a small moment of joy and comfort. But she vanished just as quickly.

And I saw Grandmother. For just a moment. The Ancient One, the elderly version who had been the biggest part of my life. What I saw of Grandmother confused me. She leaped into a portal, leaving the shimmering elf alone. When she reappeared, the elf was no longer alone, his wife at his side. His child had grown up, the wife now older. Then Grandmother vanished into another portal, a swirling vortex like the one Uncle Christopher had sent us into. Where had she gone? Was she running from my uncle? Maybe, like Mr. Winters, she would spend her life fighting, resisting until the bitter end. Watching her vanish hurt my heart. I didn't know how much more I could endure, seeing my life and the lives of those I loved pass again and again before my eyes. Madness indeed. I squeezed Noelle's hand. I squeezed Ray's. Maybe I imagined it. But for a second, it felt like they squeezed back.

Then I felt a tug.

A hard yank.

I held on tight to Ray and Noelle. I was being pulled. Slowly. Did they feel it, too? Or was I imagining it all? Maybe, like the elf kingdom, my mind was disintegrating.

Time whirled around us. My uncle reappeared. Once again, I saw the wars, the destruction, Santa cowering, the elven kingdom falling, Mr. Winters fighting, Sebwe angry, his mother weeping. It went forward. In reverse. I saw every thread of time I'd ever come in contact with. My brain felt as if it might explode.

I felt another pull. Harder this time. I heard a voice. Faint. *Swim, Carol. Like in a portal.* It was the Ancient One.

I tried to latch on to the voice. I kicked. *Swim, Noelle,* I said to Grandmother's younger self. I had to trust she could hear me. I squeezed her hand again. I squeezed Ray's. I felt hope. Fear. Strength. Resolve. I kicked and kicked. Noelle kicked, too. I could feel it now. Or sense it. And Ray felt it, too. He joined in, kicking and struggling. We began to see flashes of each other, through our visions of history. I caught a glimpse of Ray's face. "Fight," I mouthed to him, and his eyebrows scrunched in determination.

We pushed harder, like runners digging deep in the final stretch of a marathon.

We kicked and writhed.

Someone pulled.

It felt like we might never reach wherever we were going, our destination always just beyond reach. It felt as if it took forever. In a sense, it did.

But at last the whirling slowed. The flashes of history vanished. I saw a gray light in the distance. Or maybe it was right in front of me. I gave one mighty kick. Noelle and Ray did, too. I stretched. I strained. Almost.

And we tumbled out of the vortex.

Back into that hospital room.

Back into 1851.

Grandmother, her elderly self feeble and weak, stood waiting. The Ancient One screamed. Noelle screamed. The two versions merged into one. They writhed and moaned in unison. And Grandmother collapsed, shimmering from old to young, just like the time-traveling elf. She twisted in agony and I gripped her as hard as I could. The Ancient One had rescued us. But at what cost?

Ray lay beside me, his eyes open but dazed. Sebwe's mother, alone in the room, ran to the sink again, picking up the same rag with which she had dabbed our heads earlier. She dipped it into the water and knelt next to us. She held the rag to Grandmother's head. Her writhing slowly subsided.

He said it would take a few minutes for our two selves to fully merge, Grandmother said. It was one voice, weak and exhausted, but it echoed in my skull like it was two. Her hands shook. The color had drained from her face.

"Who?" I said aloud.

"The elf, dear," Grandmother responded. "He helped send me back."

"I don't understand. What happened?"

Grandmother took a deep breath. She shifted to her younger self and I shuddered. Was she damaged forever, just like the shimmering elf? "I jumped into a portal while you went back to change things. When I emerged, the elf was standing there with his wife, who was 168 years older."

I tried hard to process that. From the void, I had watched what was happening. But I hadn't fully understood it, or trusted that what I was witnessing was the true version of events. The elf and his family lived their lives from 1851 until they eventually reached 2019 where my grandmother awaited them when she came out of the portal, unaffected by my uncle's new changes. "And then you came back?" I asked.

"I made the elf help me."

"How?" I could hardly imagine that nasty elf being helpful to anyone. "He's so mean."

Grandmother smiled. "His wife knocked some sense into him. She'd had enough of your uncle's terrible world and felt guilty you were trapped where she and her son had been. But she didn't know how to get to you."

"So you came back."

"I came back."

"And how did you find us?"

"Carol, sweetie. I would go to the end of time to find you. Our connection is deep and strong. That's what love does for you. Your uncle doesn't understand that."

"Uncle Christopher!" I shouted. I scanned the room, as if he might be lurking in the shadows.

"He's not here. You know where he is."

"He left a few minutes ago," Sebwe's mother said. She dabbed Grandmother's forehead. "And he took my boy."

Grandmother shifted to her older self, the self that was weak and exhausted by the weight of life. She almost seemed defeated. Except for something in her eyes, a spark. She furrowed her ancient wrinkled brow. "Let's go get him, Carol."

"But he's too powerful," I said. "I don't think I can beat him now."

"You must. And this time, you can't let him get away."

"But I can't do it!" It wasn't that I was unwilling. I just felt certain that I couldn't win. Something had changed. He had altered history itself and put the world under his evil thumb. He had unlocked more power than anyone in history. He was like a god. Who was I to save humanity from a god?

Ray leaped to his feet. His legs wobbled, but he no longer seemed dazed. He looked angry. "Stop being a baby, Carol. YOU don't have to do it. We'll ALL do it."

"But he's so powerful, Ray."

"I don't care," he snapped. "I want my mother and father back. I want the world you told me about, a world with Santa Claus and goodness and joy. I'll die to get that."

I felt embarrassed. Of course I wanted that, too. "OK," I said. "But we have to get someone else. Another Defender." I looked at Grandmother longingly.

She knew exactly who I meant. "We'll try," she said and shifted to the young version of herself. She hopped up off the floor, full of life and energy. "I need you to use your cane to drill the hole through time. I don't think I can do it again."

"I don't have the cane," I said. "My uncle must have taken it." Grandmother's face fell.

Sebwe's mother cleared her throat. She grinned and nodded toward the bed. The subtle outline of a cane appeared under the sheet. "I grabbed it when your uncle wasn't looking," she said. "I don't like that awful man. I thought my Sebwe might be able to use it to get away from him."

I laughed and gave her a hug. I pulled the cane from under the sheet, cradling it in my arms. Having it in my possession again made me feel better about myself. Grandmother stepped next to me. I took a deep breath. "You've seen it done twice now, Carol," Grandmother said. "You think you can do it?"

"I don't know." She raised an eyebrow. "I mean, yes," I said, trying to put some steel in my voice. "I can do it!"

"Good girl." I closed my eyes and pictured how the shimmering elf did it first. Then my uncle. I tried to recall every detail, how they made their tools—the machine in the elf's case, the staff in my uncle's—spin faster and faster, in smaller and smaller circles. I slowly moved my cane before me, circling, circling, using its elven magic to amplify my power. I created a portal. The cane circled faster. The portal didn't change. Faster. Still nothing. I let out a long breath of frustration and dropped my cane. The portal collapsed.

"It's hard," I said.

"I know, dear," Grandmother responded. "I nearly killed myself finding you." She shimmered to her older self and put her wrinkled hand on mine. "You have to dig deep."

"You can do it," Ray said softly. Sebwe's mother squeezed my shoulder.

"Focus on the love you have for your father," Grandmother said. "Think of the love Ray has for his parents and the love Sebwe's mother has for her son. That's where the power will come from. Let love be your fuel."

I nodded and tried again. I squeezed Grandmother's hand and she squeezed me back and her love seemed to flow through every atom of my body. My cane spun. I opened another portal. The cane spun faster and faster. I pictured Dad's face, Ray's mother and father, Sebwe. My cane became a blur. I felt the power pulse within. I circled my hand through the air, making the vortex spin faster and drill deeper. This time it felt different. Stronger and more solid. "It's working, Carol!" Grandmother said. "Focus on your father."

I let his face float before me in my mind. I heard him call me in my memory, "Hey there, Angel Butt," as he grinned. Grandmother's eyes slammed shut. She reached toward the vortex, doing as my uncle had done, a magician conjuring something from thin air. She moved her hand left, then right, then back again. She was reaching and grabbing. She jerked her arm back. Something came spinning through the vortex. A black spot. Growing larger. I struggled to hold the vortex together. I couldn't let it collapse now. The black dot turned into a human form. I prayed it was my father. Grandmother gave one last violent pull and out shot Dad onto the hospital floor. My cane dropped. The vortex collapsed. Grandmother crumpled to the floor. And I practically leaped on top of my father, embracing him and sobbing. Dad was so dazed and confused he hugged me back, muttering, "It's OK. It's OK," though he surely had no idea who I was.

"Carol, dear, let him up," Grandmother said quietly.

I reluctantly pulled away, wiping my tears. Dad stood unsteadily. He stretched like someone waking from a long nap. He groaned and looked around. "Where am I? Who are you people?" That was like a needle in my heart. I tried to ignore it, just grateful he stood before me.

"What's the last thing you remember?" Grandmother asked.

Dad was much skinnier in this world. He looked hardened, his eyes haunted. "My brother," he answered. "We had a fight, not our first. And then he did something to me. He's strong, very powerful, and I wound up in that terrible place. I saw the world going by. Was that real?"

"I was there, too," I said. "You see different realities, different streams of time, but they're real."

"Who are you?"

The pin pricked my heart again. "I'm a friend."

This seemed to satisfy him. "I saw terrible things my brother did. Bits and pieces."

"That's why we're here," Grandmother said. "We have to stop him and we need your help."

Dad noticed Sebwe's mother. "How you're dressed." He looked around the hospital room. "This is the past, isn't it?"

"It's 1851," I answered. "When my Un . . ." I caught myself. "When your brother went back and changed things."

He looked around again. "Incredible."

"So we need to go now," I said.

"Where?"

"The North Pole," I answered. "To stop him from hurting Santa and the elves."

"Santa?" he asked. "You mean he's real?"

"Of course," Grandmother said. "And so are elves. I happen to be one of them."

Dad looked at her in disbelief. And when she shimmered from old to young, his eyes grew even wider. He seemed to be trying to convince himself that everything he was seeing and hearing wasn't some sort of illusion or fever dream, maybe the delayed effects of being in the vortex. I held my breath. Dad studied each of us. Then finally, he smiled and said, "Well, OK then. Let's go save Santa."

I grinned at him and I couldn't help myself. I gave him another big hug. He may not have known I was his daughter, his Angel Butt, but my dad, he hugged me right back.

CHAPTER 12

The Battle For the Future

"You're not about to leave me alone in this awful place," Sebwe's mother said as we prepared to make portals and execute our plan.

Grandmother put a hand on her shoulder. "But you'll be in danger, Ruth."

"Been in danger all my life," she answered. "I want to make sure nothing happens to my boy. I'm going." She crossed her arms in defiance and I had to smile. Was there any force more powerful than a parent's love for her child?

Our plan wasn't complicated, but I wasn't too happy about it either. Dad came up with it and his ruthlessness surprised me. "We have to destroy him once and for all. He'll never stop. You don't know him like I do."

I had to bite my tongue to keep from telling him I knew him plenty well and that I also knew a version of my father who would never, ever consider destroying his own brother. But I simply nodded. It wasn't as if I had any better ideas. No prison could hold my uncle. And Dad was right. He would never stop. If we didn't finish him—if *I* didn't finish him—he would finish us. Grandmother and I knew the consequences of not stopping him because they had already happened. Countless people would die or have their lives ruined in the world he created. Not to mention the terrible fate that awaited Santa. Uncle Christopher had to be destroyed, and there was a good chance I was the only one with enough power to do it. Whether Dad realized it or not, the burden fell on me.

We had to go to the North Pole to confront Uncle Christopher, and persuading Dad to use a portal took some doing. "Why not a quick jump?" he asked.

"A what?"

"A quick jump. Christopher's better at it than I am. It's like a leap through space and time over a huge distance."

"Oh, a Pole Vault," I said.

Dad looked confused, but Grandmother finally convinced him a portal was the more efficient way to travel. "We can see what we're jumping into," she said. Easy for her to say. Not being an elf, Dad would see nothing and would have to trust this odd collection of people he'd just met.

As we stood ready to go, my stomach felt as if someone were twisting it like a washcloth. I sweated like I'd been running, and it occurred to me that I hadn't had a bath in two days. I hoped I didn't stink. (Though in the smelly world of 1851, I would fit right in.)

"As soon as Mr. Glover and I are through, Carol, we'll attack," Grandmother said. "You, Ray, and Ruth follow immediately."

"OK," I said. Ray stepped up beside me and I made a portal. Grandmother and Dad stood in front of us with their backs turned. *I love you dear*, Grandmother said.

I love you, too. So much. "Good luck," I said aloud.

Grandmother made a circle in the air, and when the portal appeared and the scene at the North Pole was revealed, she and I both screamed.

Dad ducked as if something might attack him. "What?"

We already knew what had happened to the elf kingdom, of course. We'd witnessed the destruction firsthand right after Uncle Christopher had changed things. I'd also seen flashes of it from the vortex. But to watch it happening live was a horror.

Uncle Christopher and Sebwe strode through the elf kingdom like vengeful gods, blasting everything in their path. My uncle appeared to be teaching Sebwe as they went, the boy concentrating on manipulating the web around him and creating North Pulse after North Pulse. He was a quick learner, with incredible Defender gifts, and each Pulse seemed to be more powerful than the last. Chunks of shattered ice rained down on fleeing elves. Ice sculptures exploded. Elves made portals and vanished to who knows where. Other elves lay in the snow, unconscious or otherwise. Santa shielded a wounded elf. The king and queen were ushering children and the elderly through a portal when Uncle Christopher attacked from behind. Sebwe tossed blasts left and right and his eyes burned with what could only be described as madness. What had my uncle done to him? What lies had he told him about these poor creatures? I was thankful Sebwe's mother couldn't see her son.

"What's happening?" Dad repeated.

"Something terrible," I said.

"We have to go now, Carol!" Grandmother said. She grabbed Dad's hand and they leaped into the portal, landing about fifty feet away from Uncle Christopher and Sebwe. They sprinted toward the attackers. Grandmother shimmered into the younger version of herself. My uncle must have sensed a portal opening up because before Dad and Grandmother could blast him from behind, he turned. Dad flung his North Pulses, but Uncle Christopher held up his staff and deflected them. The surprise attack still staggered him, and Sebwe was knocked to the ground. The boy popped back up, his face twisted in fury.

"You need to stop, Chris," Dad shouted and fired another blast.

I adjusted my portal, drawing closer to my uncle. I wanted to emerge right on top of him and attack before he had a chance to defend himself. "Never!" he shouted, drawing back his staff.

"Now!" I screamed and the three of us jumped, hand in hand, into the fray. The cold smacked me in the face. Screams of the injured assaulted my ears. I landed a few feet from Uncle Christopher. His eyes went wide and he stumbled backward. Ray and I blasted him with North Pulses. One after the other. A relentless barrage. He partially deflected them but was thrown through the air. His staff went flying, landing ten feet from him in the snow. We fired more Pulses. Uncle Christopher threw up his hands to block them. He tried to get to his feet, but we refused to let up.

Meanwhile, Sebwe's mother grabbed her son. "Stop it, Sebwe!" she screamed. "Stop it right now." Sebwe looked stunned. The fury and madness drained from his eyes. He tried to pull away but she held him tight. She put her hands on each of his cheeks and looked him in the face. "Please, baby. Stop."

The two of them distracted me for a moment, but Dad yelled, "Finish him!" I closed in on Uncle Christopher, who crawled toward his staff. I blasted him again and he screamed, falling backward into the snow. Blood trickled from his nose. He rolled around in agony. His face had turned nearly as white as the snow in which he lay. Blood blazed crimson on his upper lip.

"Do it, Carol!" Dad yelled.

I pulled back my cane. I reached deep for the strings of time and space, shaping them into a tight ball of destruction. Of death. Ray did the same beside me. My heart thundered. Sweat felt cold against my skin. Uncle Christopher looked up. He smiled. Not a mocking smile. Not an evil one. Something almost . . . human. A tear streaked down his cheek and froze when it hit the snow. I hesitated, my cane poised above him.

"That's my girl," Uncle Christopher said. "End it." His voice was soothing, as if he were rocking an infant to sleep.

Tears spilled down my own cheeks. Ray hesitated, too, as if waiting for my cue. I trembled violently, my cane shaking in my hand. I felt nauseated. Paralyzed. I looked away from my uncle.

"I can't," I whispered.

Uncle Christopher coughed. He wiped the blood from his lip. "Do it, Carol dear."

"I can't!" I screamed. "I loved you. I still love you."

My uncle smiled again. And once more it started out as a kind smile, almost a proud one. "Of course you do," he said. Then his face slowly transformed, into anger, into hatred. "And that, Carol dear, is why I will always win." He launched himself skyward, hovering above us. We dove for cover. "Love is weakness!" he screamed. "Love is death!" And he let loose a huge North Pulse that I barely managed to block with my cane. Every bone in my body rattled. He blasted me again. And again. My cane deflected the blows. But each one hit harder than the next. One got through my defenses and struck Ray square in the chest. He screamed and gasped for breath.

Uncle Christopher laughed, floating above us. "Sebwe," he called. I scrambled away when he turned, half dragging Ray with me. Dad and Grandmother ran to help and we turned to face Uncle Christopher.

Sebwe pulled away from his mother. "No, Sebwe, no!" she shouted, collapsing in the snow. Santa crouched beside her and put his arm around her shoulder. She watched her son join Uncle Christopher, her eyes wide with fear.

Dad charged at his brother but Uncle Christopher waved his hand and Dad flew to the side, landing face first in the snow. My uncle waved his hand again and we were immobile and helpless, just as we had been in the hospital. Such an idiot I was. I should have listened to Dad and finished Uncle Christopher when I had the chance. It was the logical thing to do, the necessary thing.

Uncle Christopher floated to the ground and Sebwe joined him. He glanced nervously between us, my uncle, and his mother. Ruth reached out to him but he turned away. Santa held her close. The elf kingdom was unnaturally quiet. The elves had either vanished or were strewn about, casualties of the attack. The kingdom lay in ruins and the air smelled of smoke. The great tree still stood, not yet splintered, but an outer branch burned. The sculptures, stairs, benches, and houses lay in piles of ice, like shards of broken glass.

Uncle Christopher put his hand on Sebwe's shoulder and the boy flinched. He looked at his new protector with a mix of fear and awe. Sebwe's mother pulled herself upright. She seemed to sway on her feet and Santa steadied her. "Let this be a lesson, Sebwe," Uncle Christopher said. "Pathetic human emotions like love make you weak." Ruth took a step toward them. She bent slightly at the waist but held her head high. "Your enemies will exploit that weakness," my uncle continued. "My darling niece here is very powerful. Yet all those natural gifts will be wasted because of that one weakness. Do you under-stand?"

"Yes, sir," Sebwe said.

His mother moved closer. She stood tall and straight now and Sebwe watched her warily. Uncle Christopher turned toward her as if he might stop her advance, but Santa cleared his throat to grab my uncle's attention. Santa's suit was torn. His hat was missing. A red welt had appeared on his cheek. He brushed himself off. Snow tinkled to the Earth like fairy dust. "That's where you're wrong, Christopher."

My uncle rolled his eyes and threw back his head with a bark of laughter. "Let the lecture begin," he said. He no longer paid any attention to Ruth. "Say your piece, old man. I'll grant you that final courtesy."

Santa smiled and looked at me. "What Carol did is greater than her, Christopher. Despite all you've done, despite everything she lost because of you, she still offered mercy. She still loves you. *That* is powerful."

Uncle Christopher laughed again. "And what good will all that love and mercy do her when she's dead and gone?"

Now it was Santa's turn to laugh. "You think love dies with one person? Love is a power as great as the universe itself. It lives on and on and it will eventually triumph. Through me or Carol or someone who comes after."

Uncle Christopher held out his hands, palms up. "Are you done? Is that all you've got?"

Santa grinned slyly. "Yes, my friend. That's all I've got."

Uncle Christopher smirked. "You're no friend of mine, old man." He turned to Sebwe. "It's time. Let's do this together and you shall rule at my side and live like a king."

Sebwe hesitated, glancing at his mother. She was within a few yards of him now and stopped. "No, Sebwe," she whispered. "Please don't do it." But he and Uncle Christopher extended their hands.

I braced for the end. I was crying. Ray, too. Even Grandmother sniffled. Ruth's whole body shook. But it was the strangest thing. All Santa did was smile, as if he were doing nothing more than watching children play a silly game. Sebwe's mother looked over at him, and when she saw that smile, her shaking stopped. She stood taller.

Then she looked at me, and just like Santa, she smiled. A serene smile of such beauty that she seemed to glow, a shining star in the deepest night.

Uncle Christopher and Sebwe drew back their hands to deliver the final blows. I held my breath, perhaps my last. Dad shouted, "No, Christopher, please!"

"It's too late, dear brother," my uncle responded.

Sebwe's mother took off. She was still smiling, almost joyful. Ruth sprinted through the snow, weaving through the wreckage of ice, slipping and sliding. She leapt, beauty taking flight, a shooting star. Our two attackers flung their arms forward. Sebwe's eyes went wide at the sight of his charging mother. He jerked his arm short. Uncle Christopher was distracted, too, and his Pulse was errant, hitting us like a glancing blow.

But Sebwe's mother took the full force of her son's North Pulse. She went flying. Twenty feet or more. Landing in the snow. Sebwe screamed, like nothing I've heard before. He ran crying to her. Uncle Christopher lost his concentration and we were suddenly unfrozen. We were free.

A vortex, Carol. Grandmother's voice rattled in my brain. *Make one.* It was as if she'd drilled her idea into my thoughts. I knew exactly what I had to do. I concentrated on making the portal. Uncle Christopher's attention was on Sebwe, who knelt beside his motionless mother. The vortex I made was strong, fueled by fear and desperation. But no, it was something more than that. I could feel it. Santa was right. It was fueled by love. Love for Grandmother and Dad and Ray and poor Sebwe and his mother and what she had just done for us. Energy poured from me and through my cane. The vortex expanded. Swirling. Whirling.

Sebwe cradled his mother. Blood trickled from her nose. She was breathing, but the gasps came sporadically. Her eyes flickered open. "Mama! Mama! Are you all right? Mama!" Sebwe's cries broke my heart, but I couldn't let that distract me. I concentrated on the vortex.

"Don't be like him, baby," she whispered. "Be good."

"I'm sorry, Mama." Sebwe sobbed. He caressed her face. He kissed her forehead.

"It's OK, baby. Mama loves you." She smiled at him with such love that my heart ached to see it. I let that love flow through me.

"I love you, too, Mama." Her eyes closed. Her chest stopped its rise and fall. And she was gone. "Mama! Mama!" Sebwe screamed. He pulled her close. He shook her and kissed her. "Mama!"

"Foolish woman," Uncle Christopher said, shaking his head. "Come, Sebwe. She chose her fate."

A blast from the side knocked Uncle Christopher off of his feet. My father had circled while his brother was distracted.

Uncle Christopher pulled himself up. "You're all fools. Enough of this!" He noticed what I was doing and directed a blast my way. Ray jumped in front of me and delivered his own to deflect it. He was thrown past me and lay unmoving where he hit the ground. "You'll watch them all die before I destroy you, Carol," Uncle Christopher growled. He attacked Dad next, blowing him skyward, so high I knew he would never survive the fall. And there was nothing I could do. I had to stay focused on the vortex. Dad plummeted to Earth. All that remained were me and Grandmother and Sebwe, still sobbing and holding his mother. Uncle Christopher took aim at Grandmother next, delivering a mighty blast. But she was too quick, diving through a portal and reappearing on the other side.

Uncle Christopher laughed. "Delaying the inevitable, my elven friend. Fine, I'll just take care of my dear niece first. And that'll be that." He drew his hand back. The vortex wasn't fully formed yet. I had run out of time. He was going to win. I closed my eyes, praying for a miracle. Awaiting the final blow. "So long, Carol," he snarled.

But what came instead was a scream. Grief and rage. My eyes popped open. Sebwe was on his feet, fists clenched at his sides. Uncle Christopher glanced at him in surprise. Sebwe's arm flew back. My uncle put up his staff to shield himself. Sebwe let loose. The blast hit full force, incredibly powerful. Uncle Christopher flew backward, cartwheeling through the snow. He groaned and got to his feet. He picked up the staff that had fallen beside him. He turned to Sebwe, fury etched in every feature of his face. "I'm going to let that slide," he said. Sebwe fired another blast, staggering Uncle Christopher. But only for a second. He raised up and blasted Sebwe, who rocketed backward, landing hard.

My vortex swirled. A massive tornado of time. With one final push, I poured every ounce of energy I had through my cane. The vortex snapped into focus.

Grandmother shouted, "Now, Carol!" And she was beside me, appearing through a portal. I directed my energy toward Uncle Christopher, who was focused on Sebwe. I manipulated the threads around us, grabbing him as if I had a giant hand, lifting him in the air. He fought hard. He was still strong. I couldn't hold him for long. Uncle Christopher hovered, writhing and struggling. He managed to turn himself. He raised his staff. His face was fiery red. He pulled his arm back. But Sebwe had gotten to his feet and attacked him again. Uncle Christopher screamed and his staff landed in the snow. With the last bit of strength I could muster, I flung my uncle. Through the North Pole air. Into the vortex. Spiraling toward the place to which he'd banished us hours earlier. I watched him grow smaller and smaller, spinning and somersaulting, until he was a tiny black dot. Then he disappeared. The vortex vanished. And I collapsed in exhaustion.

I wanted to sleep, to rest for a thousand years. But Grandmother grabbed me roughly, pulling me to my feet.

"Jump, Carol!" She'd made another portal. She dragged me into it.

What are you doing? I screamed.

Just hold on. She was protecting us from something, but what? We waited once again for what seemed like forever. I felt like I was drowning. I was so drained, so exhausted, I didn't know if I would have the strength to kick my way back out once Grandmother said it was OK. At last she screamed, *Now!* I kicked feebly. Grandmother pulled me along. It seemed we'd never reach the portal opening. But we tumbled out, falling into the snow of the North Pole. Sebwe was still there, crying and holding his mother. Santa knelt beside him, embracing the sobbing boy. Some elves had returned, hugging and comforting each other. But there was no sign of Dad or Ray.

"Why did you do that?" I asked Grandmother.

"The same reason I pulled us in the first time your uncle changed history. To make sure we weren't affected. Who knows how things wound up? Hopefully everything will be back to normal when we return home."

I looked around. "But where are Dad and Ray?"

"I believe they returned to their time."

"I don't understand."

"Everything your uncle changed was undone when you threw him into the vortex. All the things he would have done from 1851 on didn't happen. Ray losing his parents and coming with us never happens. Your father being sent to the void and us pulling him out never happens. Ivan and Mr. Winters being captured never happens. If I'm right, they'll all be back in their own time and won't remember a thing."

"How can you be sure?"

"I can't. But the fact that they vanished leads me to believe I'm right."

I hoped she was, of course. But my head spun. My uncle was indeed gone. I felt certain I'd sent him into the void, where I hoped he'd stay forever and could do no more harm. But if Dad and Ray had been lost, that would be a horrible price to pay for undoing the damage Uncle Christopher had inflicted on the world.

Santa approached us with tears in his eyes. He motioned to some returning elves and they rushed over to help Sebwe and carry his mother away. The boy was inconsolable, sobbing and moaning. I felt awful for him. I wanted to hug him, to tell him things would eventually be OK. I wanted to tell him that his mother had saved not only us, but the entire world. "I'll care for him, Carol," Santa said, as if he could read my mind. "He'll do as she asked him."

"What do you mean?"

"She told him to be good," Santa said. "And he will be. I have great plans for him and others like him. He'll help me spread joy and love around the world, and he'll come to understand his mother's sacrifice and draw strength from it."

"I want to tell him I'm sorry and say goodbye."

"You can't," Grandmother said. "Hard telling how much we've messed with the future already."

"She's right, Carol," Santa said. "You've set things back to the way they were, more or less. Best to leave it alone."

"Can I hug you at least?" I asked.

Santa smiled. "Of course, Carol." I fell into his arms. His embrace was warm and soft and I wanted it to go on forever. But Grandmother tapped me on the shoulder.

"It's time," she said. Grandmother shimmered from her young self to the Ancient One. "Are you strong enough to get us back?"

"I think so." I truly was exhausted. But Santa's embrace had invigorated me. Even his touch was magical.

"And you can get us there?"

"Yes." I knew the secrets of time and space as well as the shimmering elf now. I knew how to get us home. What would await us there we could only guess.

I gave Santa a final hug and he whispered, "Thank you, Carol."

"You're welcome, Santa," I said.

I concentrated, drilling into time, into the future. I thought of Dad, sitting and chatting with Mr. Winters in Santa's house. I thought of Grandmother's cabin at the edge of the elf kingdom, a kingdom that surely would have been rebuilt 168 years from now. I thought of Santa, in all his magical glory, bringing joy to children everywhere. And after a final wave to the Big Guy, the Ancient One and I grabbed hands and stepped into the portal.

Grandmother seemed to divide into two. She grimaced and screamed, but her younger self was left behind, collapsing into the snow. Noelle smiled at us and waved farewell. The Ancient One gripped me as we traveled through time. The world rushed by in a crazy blur. I caught a glimpse of Uncle Christopher. His eyes were closed like he was sleeping. He floated in his pocket of time, there for eternity. I felt guilty but shoved those thoughts aside. That was his prison for the evil he had perpetrated. And he was alive. He was safe. My love for him and Sebwe's mother's love for her son had spared him.

When we emerged into the North Pole, I landed right on top of Grandmother in the snow. She grunted and muttered, "I'm getting too old for this nonsense." She shimmered slightly, a tiny glimpse of her younger self, but then she was back to being the Ancient One. Maybe she would be OK. The shimmering elf had made nearly a hundred trips back in time to end up the way he was. Grandmother had gone only once.

The elf kingdom stood just as we'd left it before Uncle Christopher changed everything. Elves slid down ice pathways, greeting each other in silence, their telepathic chatter filling my head. The great tree was intact, as were the houses and benches and sculptures. We turned and there stood Grandmother's cabin, looking the same as ever. I nearly collapsed with relief.

"Dad!" I shouted. "Santa!" And this time I didn't just take off running to Santa's house like a dope. I made a portal, right into the middle of Santa's living room. I dove through, Grandmother calling after me. In my haste, I landed on the living room coffee table, which happened to be filled with a tray full of cookies, mugs of hot chocolate and coffee, and a cake. Drinks flew. Cookies were squashed. The cake made a sucking sound as my shoe went right through it. Mr. Winters sat on the chair in front of me and leaped to his feet, so shocked he fell backward and nearly landed in the crackling fire. Grandmother materialized next to him and helped him to his feet.

"What in the world?" came a voice from behind me. "Angel Butt?" I turned. Dad, looking the same as ever, stared at me with utter confusion. I leaped off the table and into his arms, knocking him into his chair. I sobbed. He hugged me tight. I hugged him even tighter. "Carol, honey, what's wrong?"

"You're OK," I said. "You're OK."

"Of course I'm OK," he said, stroking my hair. "What is wrong with you? And why are you wearing that old dress?"

I'd completely forgotten I had on the dress Elizabeth had given me. I pulled back and he wiped the tears from my cheeks. I noticed the wall of toys, filled once again with playthings from every era, a history of Santa's joyful work. "Where's Santa?" I asked. "Is he safe? He's acting normal?"

"What on Earth are you talking about, Carol?" Dad asked.

Mr. Winters picked bits of cake and frosting from the front of his shirt. "I believe our young Defender has lost her marbles. Isn't that right, m'lady?"

I wanted to hug Mr. Winters, too. I wanted to laugh. But I needed to see Santa in the flesh. I needed to make sure he was all right. "Where is he?" I asked. There was no sign of Mrs. Claus either and that worried me. Did she exist? Had we accidentally changed the past and caused Santa to never meet his wife?

"He's outside," Dad said.

I pulled myself off of his lap. I had to see. But I backed into the coffee table, losing my balance, and landed butt first in what remained of the cake.

"Goodness gracious, Carol!" Dad said, laughing. "What's gotten into you?"

"I need to see him," I said desperately. "I need to see Santa."

The front door stood partially ajar. I jumped up, wiping frosting from the back of my dress. The door swung open. "I'm right here, Carol." Santa Claus! I sprinted across the room and nearly tackled him. He laughed and hugged me tight. "I'm fine, dearest," he whispered. "I'm perfectly fine. We all are, thanks to you."

I was sobbing again, looking like a fool in a weird antique dress. But I didn't care. I was so relieved. So happy. After a long hug, I finally let Santa go. And when I did, Mrs. Claus was standing behind him. I launched myself into her arms next and she rocked me back and forth. "It's OK, sweetie," she said. "Everything's OK."

That's when I noticed the sculpture, on a table next to the door. My mouth dropped open. I pulled away from Mrs. Claus to get a closer look. Carved from white marble was a teenage boy, tall and handsome. His arms were wrapped around an older woman, who looked strong and noble and wore a beautiful, serene smile. "Sebwe," I whispered. "Ruth."

"That's right, Carol," Santa said. "An eternal reminder of what they did for us."

I looked more closely. A metal plate at the bottom of the sculpture read, "Sebwe and Ruth, the First Defenders." A tear formed in the corner of my eye. Of course Ruth was a Defender. She had defended us, Santa, and the entire world. She had sacrificed herself, and because of that, Sebwe fulfilled his destiny. I felt proud to have known them.

Santa motioned to Dad and Mr. Winters. "They're here," Santa said. Dad and Mr. Winters crossed the living room, stepping carefully through spilled drinks and smashed sweets. Elves had materialized, liked they always seemed to do when work needed to be done, and were cleaning up the mess.

"Who's here?" I asked.

Santa's eyes twinkled. "Oh, just a couple of new recruits. Let's welcome them to the North Pole." Santa nudged me backward. Dad wrapped his arm around my shoulders. Mr. Winters wiped frosting from the tip of his nose and winked at me, sucking the sweetness from his finger with a loud slurp. Santa stepped away from the door. "Come on in," he called.

No one appeared for a moment but I heard whispers, urgent and unsure. And a woman's voice said, "Go on, *mi'jo*. It'll be fine." That voice sounded familiar but I couldn't place it. In stepped two boys. I nearly fainted. Then I let out a yelp of joy. Ray and Ivan-I-Am-Not stood before us, blinking in the light, side by side, as if joined at the hip. They looked confused and frightened. Especially after I knocked them both to the floor with a ferocious hug.

"You're safe! You're safe!" I squeezed them tight, crying yet again. Neither of them pushed me away, letting me hug them, maybe afraid of what I might do if they didn't.

"What is happening, Mr. Santa?" Ivan-I-Am-Not shouted. Grandmother had been right. Ivan-I-Am-Not and Ray didn't know me. They wouldn't recall any of what we'd done together. We undid all of my uncle's changes, so none of it technically ever happened. But I didn't care. *I* remembered. And I hugged them even tighter.

Santa laughed. A genuine, honest-to-goodness "Ho, ho, ho!"

"Just get used to it, boys," Santa said. "Things are always a little crazy around here."

I finally let Ray and Ivan-I-Am-Not up. Well, to be more accurate, Dad picked me up around the waist and lifted me off them. "What is happening with you, Carol?"

"It's OK," Santa said. "She has her reasons."

Dad looked at me questioningly but said nothing more. He had learned to trust Santa, even when things didn't make a lot of sense.

A light knock on the door grabbed my attention from the boys, who were dusting themselves off, as if trying to wipe away my nuttiness.

An attractive young couple stood in the doorway. It took me a second to realize who they were. The last I'd seen the man, he was lying in his front yard as the snow fell around him. And the last I'd seen her, she was being thrown into the back of a vehicle on the streets of Washington Heights. Ray's mom and dad! Another man and woman stood behind Santa, who spoke to them in a language I didn't recognize. Ivan-I-Am-Not's parents, I guessed.

I hesitated for just a moment but then thought, heck, why not? Everyone already thought I was losing it. I broke free of Dad and ran to the parents, giving them each a huge hug. They laughed, looking a little confused, but hugged me back. I pulled away and looked them in the eye. "You should be so proud of your boys," I said. "They

243

saved . . ." Grandmother cleared her throat pointedly. "They're incredibly brave."

Santa translated for Ivan-I-Am-Not's parents. They smiled and nodded their thanks. Dad gently pulled me away. "You'll have to excuse my daughter. She's not herself today."

"Oh, I don't know about that," Santa said cheerily. "Carol's never anything if not herself. Everyone, I'd like to introduce our newest Defenders, Ray and Ivan."

The boys gave shy little waves. Their parents puffed up with pride. Santa beamed. Everyone clapped. I stepped back into Dad's embrace and let his love envelop me. I thought about what Santa had said to my uncle when he was so consumed with hate, when he wanted to destroy us, the only people who had ever cared about him: "Love is a power as great as the universe itself." And I felt sad that Uncle Christopher couldn't see that, couldn't feel the kind of love we shared in this room.

And now there were two new people in my life to love and protect. I knew them and loved them already, even if they had no idea who I was and had no memory of what we'd accomplished together.

From that day forward, we would stand side by side as Defenders of Claus, protecting Santa and helping him spread joy throughout the world. And we would be friends forever, I just knew it. Because love—through time and space, through death and sorrow, through everything that can go wrong in our fragile lives—love always finds a way.

Acknowledgments

I could fill a whole book attempting to thank the people who've helped me realize my writing dreams. Creating a book is a solitary exercise, but no author makes the journey alone.

First off is my son, Tyler, who's sixteen now and way too old for my books but nonetheless is the reason I write them. He was eight when I asked him, "Would you like Daddy to write you a story?" He got excited, then I got excited and the rest is history.

My wife, Geovanny, has been nothing but supportive, and I'm grateful she never once has made an issue of how much of my time writing and publishing demands. Our pilot son Richard "took" Carol with him on his flights across the country when the first book came out. I'm so proud of him.

None of what I do would be possible without my parents, Bill and Jodi Fouch, who instilled in me the confidence and the work ethic required to be a writer. And my Christmas-obsessed Mom, of course, is the reason I chose to write about the magic of Santa. My brother, Todd, and his family are always in my corner. And according to my niece, Tierra, I'm her "second-favorite author." High praise indeed.

I'm also grateful to my Dominican family, in particular my mother-in-law, Lidia, who never fails to spoil me with rice and beans. Gracias! A special thanks to Shirleysa, whose love for the first book warms my heart. I feel like an honorary Dominican, which is why their wonderful culture finds its way into my stories.

I'm forever in debt to my agent, Jennifer Unter, who's always there when I need her (which is way too often). My editor at Sky Pony, Nicole Frail, has been unwavering in her enthusiasm and has guided me through some rough waters. I'd also like to thank my previous editors, Bethany Buck and Becky Herrick, who helped bring Carol to life. And a huge thanks to Sky Pony for sending Carol out into the world.

I need to thank the members of my writing group, Stephanie Fitzpatrick, Barbara Senenman, Sue Henn, and Rosanne Matty, for helping make my books better. A tip of the cap to David Miles for another amazing cover illustration. My hometown hero JoAnn Harman has worked tirelessly to support me and my books. And thanks to Kevin Amorim, who listens patiently whenever I subject him to my wacky story ideas.

Most of all, I want to express my gratitude to all the kids out there who've made Carol a small part of their lives. Occasionally I'll hear a cranky grown-up complain about "these kids today" and their devices and their social media and on and on. That's bunk. The children I've encountered during school visits and events are ten times smarter than I ever was at their age. Like Carol, they're going to save the world.